A Series Of Small Shocks Rippled Down Her Spine. Those Eyes.

That deep golden tint. The russet outer ring around the dark iris. Wolf's eyes, the former librarian in her cataloged automatically, due to the high incidence of that color in wolves.

Like… Like…

Like the eyes that had haunted her dreams for years. Mocking her. Taunting her to shed her prissy inhibitions. Tempting her to sin.

It couldn't be him! This high-powered executive *couldn't* be the hot stud she'd given her virginity to. The bastard who'd roared out of her life the next morning, leaving a trail of devastation in his wake.

She couldn't breathe, couldn't think as he approached. Those wolf's eyes never left her face.

"Hello, Caroline. It's been a long time."

Dear Reader,

My husband and I have stumbled across some magical spots during our many years of rambling. Tossa de Mar, on Spain's Costa Brava, ranks right up near the top of our list. We found it by chance during a jaunt that took us from Madrid to Seville to Barcelona to the Strait of Gibraltar.

When we stopped in Tossa, I fell instantly in love with its sparkling bay, crescent-shaped beach and ancient ruins. What made it even more special is that Al and I celebrated an anniversary there. So when I needed a spot to set the stage for *The Executive's Valentine Seduction,* I knew it had to be beautiful Tossa by the Sea—especially since this book comes out during the celebration of Harlequin's 60th Anniversary.

I'm thrilled to be part of that celebration. Congratulations to Harlequin Books for providing six decades of romance, intrigue, inspiration and adventure!

All my best,

Merline

MERLINE LOVELACE

THE EXECUTIVE'S VALENTINE SEDUCTION

Published by Silhouette Books
America's Publisher of Contemporary Romance

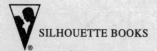

SILHOUETTE BOOKS

ISBN-13: 978-0-373-76917-9
ISBN-10:   0-373-76917-2

Recycling programs
for this product may
not exist in your area.

THE EXECUTIVE'S VALENTINE SEDUCTION

Visit Silhouette Books at www.eHarlequin.com

Printed in U.S.A.

MERLINE LOVELACE

A retired air force officer, Merline Lovelace served at bases all over the world, including tours in Taiwan, Vietnam and at the Pentagon. When she hung up her uniform for the last time, she decided to combine her love of adventure and flair for storytelling, basing many of her tales on her experiences in the service.

Since then, she's produced more than seventy-five action-packed novels, many of which have made the *USA TODAY* and Waldenbooks bestseller lists. Over ten million copies of her works are in print in thirty-one countries. Named Oklahoma's Writer of the Year and the Oklahoma Female Veteran of the Year, Merline is also a recipient of the Romance Writers of America's prestigious RITA® Award.

Check Merline's Web site at www.merlinelovelace.com for news, contests and information about upcoming releases. And be sure to watch for *The Hello Girl,* a heart-warming story of love that spans time, coming soon from Harlequin Books.

For my darling,
who explored Tossa de Mar with me all those years ago.
I can't wait for all the adventures yet to come!

One

Caroline Walters had no premonition her world was about to implode that balmy February afternoon.

She stood in the lobby of a new, upscale resort in Tossa de Mar, a seaside vacation spot on Spain's Costa Brava, just an hour north of Barcelona. While Caro breathed in the fragrance of the bloodred gladiolas on the table beside her, she waited for the silver BMW gliding along the palm-lined drive to pull up at the resort's entrance.

The big moment was finally here. Her first meeting with the client who'd had her and her two partners jumping through hoops for the past month!

She used the final few seconds before he arrived

to check the mirror framing the gladiolas. Her honey-brown hair was smooth, with not a single tendril escaping from the heavy twist. Her green eyes gazed back at her with just the right degree of confidence. Her slim, black wool crepe skirt and matching jacket didn't show a single wrinkle.

Satisfied she looked the part of a coolly compe-tent travel consultant and event coordinator, she flipped through the embossed leather folder she'd prepared for Rory Burke, founder and chief execu-tive of the LA-based firm Global Security, Inc. She wanted to make sure she'd included everything Burke had requested.

Final conference agenda, check.

Resort layout, check.

Diagrams showing room setup for general ses-sions, check.

Additional diagrams for breakout rooms, check.

Arrival times and room numbers of all attend-ees, check.

Burke's hotel preregistration and room key, check.

Reassured everything was in place, Caroline closed the folder. She was primed and ready.

She should be! She and her partners had worked their buns off since this short-notice job dropped in their laps a few days before Christmas. They'd had just a little over a month to scout locations and pull together a conference plan for the hundred-plus security agents flying in from all parts of the world.

January had passed in a blur of frantic prep work. The flurry of e-mails and phone calls with Burke's people had multiplied exponentially the first week in February. Two days ago Caro had flown to Spain to nail down the final details. In several marathon sessions with the resort's conference coordinator, she'd reconfirmed menus, special dietary considerations, room setups and audiovisual aids.

She'd also tackled the rather daunting challenge of arranging a demo facility for an assortment of lethal weapons. In a last-minute change to the conference agenda, Global Security's head honcho had added a hands-on session to test new offensive and defensive weaponry for the protection of their clients.

As its name implied, GSI specialized in providing threat analysis and personal protection for clients ranging from kings and rock stars to newspaper editors who landed on religious fanatics' hate lists. The company profile indicated its agents were drawn from the ranks of military and law enforcement in twelve different countries.

The company's CEO was equally fascinating. His bio read like a James Bond novel. U.S. Army Ranger. Special Ops duty in war-torn Bosnia. A short stint with an unspecified government agency. Advisor to the Columbian Presidential Protection Unit. Founder and chief operating officer of GSI. Now fielding highly specialized agents in Iraq, Darfur, Indonesia,

Latin America—just about every hot spot on the globe.

Somewhere along the way he'd also managed to complete a bachelor's degree in law enforcement and a master's degree in international affairs. Curiously, neither his bio nor his company Web site had included a photo of Burke or any of his operatives. Caro suspected that might have something to do with GSI's pledge to provide "complete, confidential and anonymous protection."

As a former librarian, Caroline had read more than her share of action/adventure novels. She could admire real-life James Bond types like Rory Burke. Unfortunately, her one brief walk on the wild side had produced such disastrous consequences that she had *zero* desire to emulate their exploits.

So she couldn't help feeling both curious about and just a touch wary of her new client. She didn't allow either emotion to show, however, as the rental car she'd reserved for him at the Barcelona Airport pulled under the resort's vine-covered portico. A polite smile firmly in place, she waited while he exited the BMW and strode through the double glass doors.

Her first thought was that Burke certainly fit the mental image she'd constructed in her head. Despite the pinstripes and Italian silk tie, he wasn't someone she wanted to encounter in a dark alley.

The hand-tailored suit only emphasized his lean, rangy build. He wore his tawny hair cut ruthlessly short. His nose was flattened at the bridge, as if it had taken a direct hit from a club or a gun butt. And when he peeled off his mirrored sunglasses, his amber eyes lasered into Caro.

A series of small shocks rippled down her spine. Those eyes. That deep golden tint. The russet outer ring around the iris. Wolf's eyes, the former librarian in her cataloged automatically, due to the high incidence of that color in wolves.

Like... Like...

Like the eyes that had haunted her dreams for years. Mocking her. Taunting her to shed her prissy inhibitions. Tempting her to sin.

Her heart stuttered. Her breath sliced like a razor blade inside her throat.

It couldn't be him! This high-powered executive *couldn't* be the young tough whose motorcycle she'd climbed aboard one steamy summer night. The hot stud she gave her virginity to. The bastard who'd roared out of her life the next morning, leaving a trail of devastation in his wake.

She couldn't breathe, couldn't move, couldn't think as he approached. Those wolf's eyes never left her face.

"Hello, Caroline. It's been a long time."

Oh God! Oh God, oh God, oh God!

Her mind reeled with disbelief. Everything in her shouted a denial. She gouged her nails deep into her palms and felt her body go ice-cold then blaze white-hot when Burke shot out a hand to grip her upper arm.

"But don't keel over on me."

The gruff command triggered the survival instincts Caro had been forced to develop in the aftermath of that long-ago night. She couldn't quite stop the trembling, but she clamped down on the waves of dizziness and dragged in a breath that cut like jagged glass.

"How…? When…?"

"When did I find out I got you pregnant?" he finished for her. "Three months ago."

His gaze swept the lobby, came back to her.

"This isn't the place to discuss the result of our one-night stand. Let's take it somewhere private. Am I preregistered?"

"I… Uh…" She swiped her tongue over dry lips. "Yes."

"You have the room key?"

She could only nod this time.

"What's the room number?"

"Five…" She forced herself to breathe, to think. "Five oh eight."

He waited to relay the number to the bellman wheeling in his luggage before steering Caro toward the elevators. His hand remained locked around her upper arm. His body crowded hers in the claustrophobic cage.

She didn't say a word on the way up. She was still numb with shock, still fighting desperately to suppress the emotions that bombarded her.

She'd thought she'd put her past behind her. Was so certain she'd wiped out every remnant of her paralyzing fear when she finally realized she was pregnant, her shame at having to drop out of high school, her despair of being bundled off to a haven for pregnant teens.

She'd never gotten over the heartache of delivering a stillborn, seven-month-old baby, however. That stayed with her always. The experience had molded her into the woman she was today. Quiet. Contained. Careful.

And strong, she reminded herself grimly. Strong enough to survive. Strong enough to endure. Certainly strong enough to deal with Rory Burke.

Rory Burke. The name fit the man he'd become, but in no way could she connect it to the cocky, T-shirted eighteen-year-old who'd worked in her uncle's garage for a few weeks that long-ago summer.

"I never knew your real name," she got out through frozen lips as they exited the elevator. "My uncle and cousin always called you Johnny. Or Hoss."

Short for Stud Hoss, her shamefaced cousin had admitted later. By then it was too late.

"John—Johnny—is my middle name. I stopped

using it when I went into the army. The military isn't big on calling recruits by their middle names. Or *any* name except some that can't be repeated in polite company." He stopped at a set of double doors. "Five oh eight. This is it."

She fumbled in the leather folder for the key card. All her careful work—the agenda, the layout, the support setups—went unnoticed as Burke slipped the card into the lock and stood aside for her to precede him.

She'd checked out the lavish four-room suite just a half hour ago. The welcome basket still sat on the slab of polished granite that served as a coffee table. The handwritten note from the resort manager was still propped beside it. The minibar was stocked with single malt scotch, Burke's reported drink of choice. Yet Caro was too numb to absorb any of the details she'd checked so meticulously.

She dropped the leather folder on the coffee table beside the basket. With her arms wrapped around her waist, she turned to the man she'd never expected to see again.

"You said…"

She stopped, cringing at the ragged edge in her voice. She wasn't a frightened seventeen-year-old, dammit! She'd survived the angry recriminations her parents had thrown at her. All those lonely weeks at the home. The wrenching loss of her baby.

In the process, she'd discovered a strength she

didn't know she had. That inner core had pushed her to finish high school by correspondence, work her way through college and attend grad school on a full scholarship. During her junior year in college, she met the two women who would become her closest friends and, ultimately, her business partners. She'd built a life for herself. She owed no explanations to anyone, least of all this man.

But he sure as hell owed her one!

"You said you just found out three months ago I got pregnant."

"That's right."

"How?"

He tossed the key card on the coffee table and yanked at the knot of his tie. "I had dinner with a prospective client. Turns out his wife's from Millburn."

Millburn, Kansas. Population nine thousand or so. The town where Caro had spent the first seventeen years of her life. The town she'd returned to only once in the years since she'd left—for her father's funeral.

"The wife's name is Evelyn Walker," Burke said as he slid the tie from around his neck with a slither of silk on starched cotton. "Maiden name was Brown. Maybe you remember her?"

"Oh, yes. I remember Evelyn Brown."

They'd never been friends. They'd rarely talked to each other in the halls at school. But Evelyn had led the chorus of smirks and snide comments when word leaked that prim, prissy Caroline Walters had gotten herself knocked up.

"I asked the woman if she knew you."

His eyes held hers. Those compelling, dangerous eyes that had made Caro shiver every time he'd looked her over all those years ago.

"She told me you dropped out of high school at the start of your senior year. She also told me why."

"Schools weren't as tolerant of teenage pregnancies back then as they are today."

She could say it without bitterness. She'd never blamed the guidance counselor who'd called her in and told her she had to leave. Never blamed her parents for shipping her off to live with strangers. *She* was the one who'd tossed aside every principle, every precaution drummed into her by parents, teachers and church pastors to climb aboard a motorcycle that sweltering summer night.

"When I heard what happened, I…"

A brusque knock cut into Burke's terse explanation. With a muttered oath, he went to let in the porter with his luggage.

Caro grabbed at the interruption with relief. She turned to stare through the doors that gave onto a wide balcony. The spectacular views had mesmerized her when she was scouting locations for the GSI conference last month. Now she barely registered the medieval castle brooding high on a rocky promontory at the far end of a perfect, crescent beach.

Tourists strolled the wide seawall circling the beach, admiring the remnants of a walkway first laid by the Romans when Hispania was one of its far-flung provinces. Several fishermen sat beside boats drawn up onto the sandy shore, mending their nets in close proximity to the few hearty sun worshippers stretched out on towels or blankets.

It was a picture-postcard scene, one Caro was in no mood to appreciate. But staring at the endless stretch of sky and sea gave her time to squelch her churning emotions before she faced Burke again.

"So Evelyn told you I was pregnant. Do you want to know what happened to the baby?"

"I know what happened. I ran a check of birth certificates."

Birth and death. One and the same for the stillborn baby she'd buried; only the sympathetic manager of the home was beside her.

She fought to keep the bleak memory at bay, but Burke must have seen it in her eyes. He crossed the room and stretched out a hand.

Caro's tight hold on her emotions left no room for touching. She jerked back, and he dropped his arm.

"I'm sorry you had to go through that all alone," he said quietly. "If I'd known, I would have come back to Millburn."

That surprised her. Even more surprising was the fact that he didn't ask if he was the father.

Then again, he knew she was a virgin that night. He had to, given her inexperienced fumbling and surprised yelp when he penetrated her. Then, of course, there was the blood he'd wiped from her thighs with his wadded T-shirt.

"My uncle tried to contact you," Caroline said stiffly, "but he'd always paid you in cash, under the table. He didn't know your Social Security number. Or your real name for that matter. We had no way of tracking you down."

"I'm sorry," he said again.

She knew in her heart it wouldn't have made any difference if he *had* come back. Chances were she still would have lost the baby. And she still would have had to live with her parents' bitter disappointment in her.

"I'm sorry, too. I won't lie to you. The experience changed my life in ways I could never have imagined back then. I was so young, so stupidly naive. But in the end, it made me stronger."

She lifted her chin. This time it was her gaze that held his, direct and unflinching.

"I've put the past behind me. I suggest you do the same."

"That might be difficult, seeing as it just caught up with me a few months ago."

"Try," she snapped. "Try very hard. We're going

to be working together for the next five days. I don't want to…"

She broke off, her eyes widening.

"Oh God! I didn't connect the dots until this moment." Disgusted, she shook her head. "The conference… This job… It dropped in our laps just a little over a month ago. *After* you found out about me."

"I checked you out," he admitted without a trace of apology. "Saw you'd quit your job at the library to launch this business with your two partners. I also saw you sank your entire savings into start-up costs and nationwide advertising. That wasn't real smart," he added in an aside, "considering the three of you could have qualified for a small, woman-owned business loan and kept your personal assets intact."

She brushed over his editorial comment in her outrage over this invasion of her privacy. "How did you get that kind of information?"

"I'm in the security business, remember? I have access to all sorts of databases."

"You had no right to delve into my personal life or my finances!"

"Wrong." His mouth took a wry twist. "I've broken pretty well every rule in the book over the years, but there are a couple I live by. One, I keep my back to the wall. Two, I pay my debts."

Caro didn't think she figured into rule number one. That left number two.

A healthy dose of anger swept through her, scattering the other emotions this man had roused. She wasn't a shy, uncertain teenager anymore! She hadn't been for a long, long time. Becoming the butt of so many malicious jokes and whispers had stripped away her natural shyness and fired an inner core of tempered steel.

"Let's get one thing straight, Burke. You don't owe me a thing. You didn't drag me down to the river that night and have your way with me. I went with you willingly."

Willingly, hell! She'd been so eager, so hungry for the muscled-up kid with the wicked grin and daredevil glint in his eyes that she could hardly think that summer, much less weigh the consequences.

"Whatever price had to be paid for that bit of idiocy I paid long ago. The slate's clean."

"Not hardly."

He reached for her again, giving her no chance to flinch away this time. His fingers tipped her chin. His eyes narrowed as they locked with hers.

"Millburn was just a brief stop on a road that would have landed me in jail sooner or later. I'd probably be behind bars now if I hadn't gotten crosswise of a cop who grabbed me by the scruff of the neck and dragged me to an Army recruiter instead of the police station."

She'd sensed that in him. The recklessness. The hint of danger. They'd only added to his appeal. Prim, proper Caroline Walters had been seduced as much by the age-old desire to taste forbidden fruit as by a pair of tight jeans.

"You said what you went through changed your life," he said grimly. "The Army changed mine. Saved it, I guess you could say. In return, I gave everything I had to my platoon every minute I was in uniform. And when I got out, I went back and found the cop who kicked my ass all those years ago. Harry's now my senior VP of operations."

His thumb brushed the curve of her chin. His compelling amber eyes telegraphed a message she couldn't begin to interpret.

"It's your turn, Caroline. One way or another, I intend to make things right with you."

Two

Rory could see he'd rocked his consultant back on her heels. No surprise there. He'd taken a few hits himself since learning he'd fathered a child in a single, irresponsibly careless act.

The woman who'd had to live with the consequences of that act frowned up at him now. Her heart-shaped face was a study in distrust and disbelief. Her forest-green eyes reflected her fierce struggle to deal with the shock of his unexpected reappearance in her life.

"I… I need some air. I'll let you get settled in. We can talk later."

They'd do more than talk. Rory had already

decided that. But he would give her the space she needed to recover before initiating the next phase of his campaign.

"I'm still on U.S. time," he reminded her. "How about an early dinner? Six o'clock?"

"Okay. Sure. Fine."

"I'll meet you in the bar downstairs."

With a distracted wave, she indicated a leather portfolio on the coffee table. "The conference information is in that folder. I'll see you later."

She certainly would. Rory hadn't spent all those years in the Army without learning to develop contingency plans for just about every situation. He'd put a good deal of time and thought into Operation Caroline Walters.

As the door closed behind her, he tried to reconcile the woman she'd become with the seventeen-year-old she'd been. It took some doing. His memory of that summer was a little hazy around the edges.

With good reason. He'd left home at sixteen after a final, explosive brawl with his drunk of a father. For more than a year he'd drifted across the country on the beat-up Ducati 600 he'd put together from spare parts, picking up odd jobs as he went. Best he could recall, he'd worked for less than a month in the garage owned by Buck Walters. Millburn, Kansas, was too flat, too dusty and way too boring for his taste.

The same couldn't be said about Walters's niece. Rory vaguely remembered a shy smile, an embarrassed blush whenever he caught her eye and *very* shapely legs showing beneath her shorts.

The legs had interested him a whole lot more than her smiles or blushes. He'd been such a horny bastard at that age. Most of the time he'd walked around with a permanent hard-on. So naturally he'd had to strip off his T-shirt whenever the shy brunette came into her uncle's garage. Had to tease a smile out of her. Had to taunt her into a ride on the Ducati.

He'd never really expected her to swing into the saddle behind him the night before he left town. Never dreamed she'd wrap her arms around his waist and lean into his back that hot August evening. And when they'd parked beside the river, he sure as hell had never expected to get lucky.

The next morning, he remembered with a grimace of disgust, he'd left with a casual promise to call the next time he came anywhere close to Kansas. Thirteen years later, he still hadn't been back.

But he was here. Now. With the woman whose life he'd altered so irrevocably that night.

Her stricken look when she confirmed the pregnancy made Rory want to kick himself all over again for not using a condom. Or maybe he had and the damned thing didn't work. All he knew for sure was Buck Walters's niece didn't sleep around. Not back then, anyway. She'd given him ample proof of that.

He'd covered a lot of miles since that night and been with his share of women. As far as he knew, he'd never left one crying or cursing his name. The fact that he'd given Caroline plenty of reason to do both had scratched at Rory's conscience, big-time.

He'd begun developing Operation Caroline Walters the day after he'd learned of her pregnancy. His first objective had been to scope out the target. That hadn't taken long. A few clicks of the keyboard and some poking around in databases he had legal access to—and several he didn't—had verified the basic facts.

His second objective was to arrange the initial contact. He'd debated whether to approach her on a personal basis or through her business. He'd opted for the business angle for two strategic reasons. One, it gave him a hold over her. She couldn't just haul off, slug him in the jaw and stalk away. Second, this angle dovetailed nicely with his corporate plans. With so many explosive events happening all around the world, he'd been planning to pull in his key operatives for a face-to-face.

The third objective involved actually making the contact. Rory could now check that item off his plan. The meeting had gone pretty much as he'd scripted. Except...

He'd expected to experience a welter of emotions when he saw her again. Guilt, yes. Regret, certainly. Relief that he'd taken the first steps to making things right for the girl whose life he'd brought crashing down around her ears, for sure.

But he *hadn't* expected this tug of interest in the woman that girl had become. He'd shocked the hell out of her; yet she hadn't folded, hadn't yielded an inch of ground. This Caroline Walters was tougher than the shy girl he remembered. Tougher than those misty green eyes and soft mouth would lead a man to expect.

Then, of course, there were those smooth, silky legs.

The sudden tightening in his groin had Rory shaking his head in disgust. He wasn't a horny young stud anymore. He'd learned to control his appetites and harness his lust.

Stick to the plan, man! Keep the final objective firmly in view.

With that stern admonishment, he popped the buttons on his shirt and headed for the shower to sluice off the effects of his transatlantic flight.

Caro wanted out of the resort.

She had to escape the confines of her mini-suite. Had to hit the paved walkway circling the beach and let the stiff sea breeze blow away some of her shock and confusion.

She also needed to contact her partners. She had to advise them of this incredible development and get their take on how the heck she should proceed with Rory Burke. Deciding she could talk and walk, Caro dug her cell phone out of her purse and tucked it in her jacket pocket with her room key.

The salt breeze slapped into her the moment she exited the resort's lower level. February wasn't the warmest month on this stretch of Spain's Costa Brava. That didn't deter the determined sun worshippers who flocked from more northern climates to soak up the Mediterranean rays, however. Caro picked up snatches of German, Swedish, French and Russian as she set off along the tiled walk first laid by the Romans.

An elderly Spaniard in a sweater vest and black beret hunched on the seawall, a cigarette dangling from his lips. He stared out to sea with eyes narrowed in his weathered face and displayed no interest in the topless bather stretched out on the beach below. Her generously siliconed breasts had certainly attracted the interest of others, though. Caro had to skirt a small crowd of tourists, all male and all avidly clicking away with their cameras.

Caroline found a sheltered spot at the base of the hill leading up to the castle ruins. Perching on the seawall, she pulled out her cell phone. Luckily, both of her partners were currently in Europe so she didn't have to juggle time zones. Devon McShay had arrived in London just this morning with Cal Logan. The CEO of Logan Aerospace now had her handling all his European connections.

Sabrina Russo was in Rome, busy setting up a satellite office and sorting through an avalanche of potential jobs steered her way by the handsome neurosurgeon she'd fallen for—literally and figuratively!—last month.

Caro speed-dialed Sabrina first and felt her heart lift at just the sound of her friend's cheerful greeting.

"Hey, girl. Wazzup?"

"Hang on a sec. I want to get Dev on the line for a three-way."

She hit the button for a conference call and caught Devon in a limo with Cal Logan, on their way to a meeting with British Aerospace.

"Hi, Caro."

"Hi, Dev. Sabrina's on the line, too."

"Great. I need to update you both on my itinerary. But first… Did you get our new client all meeted and greeted?"

"Yes."

Caro kept her voice even, or thought she did, but the other two women had known her too long. Both picked up on the clipped response.

"Uh-oh. Is there a problem?"

"You could say that."

She couldn't think of any way to break the news except to blurt it out.

"Rory Burke, Global Security's chief exec, is the father of the baby I lost when I was in high school."

Simultaneous exclamations burst through the phone.

"What!"

"No way!"

"Trust me, you're not half as flabbergasted as I was. Still am, for that matter. I'm—I'm not sure how to handle this."

"You don't have to handle it," Sabrina shot back. "You pack up, girlfriend. Right now. Catch the next flight home. I'll zip over from Rome and deliver a hard, swift kick to the bastard's balls before orchestrating the rest of his friggin' conference."

"That'll bring us a lot of future business," Caro said on a shaky laugh.

"We don't need Burke's business," Devon added with equal fervor. "I'm with 'Rina. Tell the jerk to take a long walk off a short pier, and get out of there."

Caro had to put in reluctant protest. "He's not a total jerk. He didn't know I was pregnant. I never told him."

"Because you couldn't find him!"

Their fierce, unquestioned loyalty eased some of the tightness in Caroline's chest. Devon and Sabrina were her best friends as well as business partners. The *only* friends she'd ever opened up to about her past.

She'd met them for the first time at the University of Salzburg, where they'd shared rooms while participating in a Junior Year Abroad Program. Still carrying the emotional scars from high school, Caro had been distant and reserved at first.

The combination of a minuscule apartment, Sabrina's bubbling personality and Devon's passionate love of all things historical had gradually penetrated her shield. Looking back, Caro would always zero in on that year in Salzburg as the point where she came fully alive again.

Now the three of them were in business together. Partners in a fledgling company called European Business Services, Inc.—EBS for short. Since EBS launched last year they'd kept busy providing travel, translation and support services for executives doing business in Europe. Caro had thoroughly enjoyed the clients she'd worked with so far.

This one, though, was in a class by himself.

"Thanks for the moral support," she told her friends with heartfelt sincerity.

"Moral support, hell!" Sabrina grumbled. "I still want to kick some gonads."

"Hold on to that thought," Caro said with a faint smile. Talking through her shock and confusion like this had provided just the shot in the arm she needed. "I appreciate your offer to do the dirty for me but…"

Her gaze shifted to the waves rolling in to the beach. They were endless. Relentless. Like time. Like her past. The only way to deal with it, the only way Caro knew to deal with any problem, was to face it head-on.

"If there's any gonad-kicking to be done," she told her partners, "I'll do it myself."

"You sure you don't want one of us to fly in?" Devon asked, sounding worried and unconvinced.

"I'm sure. I just needed to talk to you guys and let you know there might be a problem with this contract."

She managed to inject more confidence into the calm reply than she was feeling. *Much* more.

"Whatever you decide," Sabrina reminded her unnecessarily, "Dev and I are behind you two thousand percent. Stay in Spain, don't stay. Deck the bastard, don't deck him. Just keep us posted, okay?"

"I will."

Caro flipped the cell phone shut, feeling a hundred pounds lighter and a hundred years younger. She couldn't erase the memories of that awful time. She would live with them forever. But she didn't have to let them cloud her future.

She was in control of her life, she reminded herself sternly. What's more, she was part owner in a firm with a very lucrative contract on the line.

She would use the hours until dinner to shake off the residual effects of coming face-to-face with her past and figure out a way to smooth over this awkward situation. When she met Rory Burke this evening, she vowed she would be cool, calm and completely professional.

Cool and calm went up in smoke two seconds after Caro spotted her client in the resort's trendy bar.

He had a drink in front of him—scotch she presumed, since that's what his administrative assistant had told her to stock his suite with—and was crunching down on an appetizer from the assortment arrayed on the cocktail table.

He must have showered before coming down. Dampness still glistened in his dark blond hair. He was also, Caro saw with a jolt that went through her entire system, wearing a black V-neck sweater and faded jeans. Both items molded a body far more mature and muscled than the one she remembered.

She'd prepped for another meeting with the smooth, polished executive, dammit. She'd rehearsed what she would say, had her conditions for continuing their professional relationship all laid out. Her prepared speech didn't fit the man who rose and strode over to her.

He was too relaxed, too informal and far too dangerous. She didn't trust his easy smile. *Or* her instinctive reaction to it.

"I ordered some *tapas*." He gestured to the colorful display on the table. "Care to indulge?"

"When in Spain…" Caro murmured, trying once again to recover her balance. Rory Burke seemed to be making a habit of throwing her off it.

"What would you like to drink?"

"White wine. Godello, if they have it."

"I'll bring it to the table."

Caroline had spent enough time in Spain to identify most of the appetizers on the small cocktail table. Spaniards had a passion for *tapas,* flavorful bite-size bits that served more as a conduit for socializing in bars and restaurants after work than a source of nourishment.

There were as many variations of *tapas* as there were cooks. The dozen or so small dishes in front of her held aromatic combinations of chickpeas and spinach, clams in sherry paprika sauce, roasted almonds, fried calamari, olives, red peppers with anchovies, garlic shrimp and what looked like chunks of cod wrapped in grape leaves, all staked with wooden toothpicks for easy nibbling.

Paprika seared her palate after one bite of the clams. With her tongue on fire, she reached for the wine Burke brought her with a murmur of fervent thanks. Before she could take a sip, he'd reclaimed his seat and raised his own glass.

"Shall we drink to new beginnings?"

That stopped the wine halfway to Caro's lips. Her eyes met his across the small table. She couldn't interpret the message in their amber depths, but common courtesy demanded she at least acknowledge his toast. Her burning tongue made that courtesy a necessity.

"To new beginnings."

The tangy, light-bodied Godello extinguished the paprika-fueled fire. Able to draw breath again, Caro set down her glass and launched into her prepared spiel.

"Okay, here's the deal. I've spent the time since your arrival trying to decide how best to handle this situation."

"I expect you have."

"First, I don't appreciate the backhanded way you arranged this…this reunion."

He hooked a brow. "You don't appreciate that I dropped a fat contract in your lap?"

"You should have been up-front with me. Told me who you were."

"I didn't try to hide my identity," he countered mildly. "My name is on the contract."

"You knew darn well I would never associate the chief executive officer of GSI with the kid everyone, including my uncle and cousin, called Johnny."

"Would you have taken the job if I'd spelled it out for you?"

"Probably not. And that brings us to the conditions under which I'll continue to work this conference for you."

She edged several of the small dishes aside. Hands clasped loosely on the table, she kept her gaze steady and her tone even.

"I don't want any further discussion of our previous association. Nothing either of us can say will change what happened, so there's no need to rehash it. Agreed?"

He toyed with a tooth-picked clam, trailing the succulent morsel through the dark sherry sauce. Caro glanced down to follow the movement and found herself wondering when and how he'd acquired those thin, faded scars webbing across the back of his hand.

"Agreed," he said after a moment. "As you said, we can't change what happened."

"And this notion that you have to make things right with me… Forget it. There's nothing to make right. I'm content with my life now. Very content. I don't want you charging into it out of some mistaken sense of obligation."

"All right. I won't charge."

Her eyes narrowed in suspicion. The reply was too amiable, too quick.

"Let me rephrase that. I don't want you in my life, period."

"Too late for that," he said reasonably. "I'm here. You're here. We'll be working together for the next four days."

"Then I want your agreement that's all we'll do," she stated emphatically. "Work."

The clam made another slow swirl. He contemplated its dark trail for a few seconds before lifting those russet-ringed eyes to hers.

"I can't promise you that. Who's to say the heat that flared between us back in Millburn won't ignite again? But I can promise this," he added as she went as stiff as a board, "I won't make the same mistakes I made then. And I won't make any moves you don't want me to. You're safe with me, Caroline. I swear it."

"Yeah, right," she muttered. "Isn't that what the big, bad wolf said to Little Red Riding Hood?"

He grinned then, looking so much like the cocky kid she'd mooned over all those years ago that her heart knocked against her ribs.

"Pretty much," he agreed.

Three

Caroline was up at six-thirty the next morning. Since most of the GSI attendees were coming in from the field, their CEO had specified casual attire. Caro had to walk a fine line as the event coordinator, however. Jeans and jungle boots wouldn't hack it for her.

She settled instead on dove-gray slacks and a wide-sleeved cotton tunic in warm tangerine paired with the colorful espadrilles she'd picked up in Tossa de Mar's open-air market. Winding her hair up into its usual neat twist at the back of her head, she anchored it with a clip. A few swipes of blush and a quick pass with lip gloss and she was done.

She rechecked her zippered conference file for the fifth or sixth time. Satisfied she had everything she needed, she hit the door. With the conference set to kick off at eleven, she'd arranged a breakfast meeting with her GSI focal point to go over last-minute details. Caro and Harry Martin had exchanged dozens of e-mails over the past two months. She'd kept hers brisk and businesslike. His had been so succinct as to be almost indecipherable. A man of few words, Harry Martin.

And, according to Rory's startling revelations yesterday, he was the man who'd hauled a smart-mouthed kid into an Army recruiter's office all those years ago and put his life back on track. After what Rory had told her about his senior VP of operations, Caro expected a big, grizzled retired cop.

Martin was definitely big. Six-three or -four at least. He had to stoop to avoid brushing the grapevines that dangled from the arbor leading to the terrace restaurant. Grizzled, he wasn't. Sleek Ray-Bans shielded his eyes above chiseled cheeks and a serious, unsmiling mouth. His khakis sported a knife-blade crease, and his sky-blue polo shirt stretched across a frame that looked fit and trim. His salt-and-pepper buzz cut gave the only clue to his age.

"Ms. Walters?" He set a notebook on the table and folded her hand in a tough, callused palm. "Harry Martin."

"Good to finally meet you, Mr. Martin."

"Harry," he corrected as he seated himself at the umbrella-shielded table. "Caroline okay with you?"

"Of course. How was your flight from Casablanca?"

She knew he'd flown into Morocco two days ago and from there to Barcelona late last night.

"Fine."

He helped himself to coffee from a stainless-steel carafe and proceeded to dump five heaping spoonfuls of sugar into his cup. Wondering how the heck he managed to stay so trim, Caro watched with some fascination as he stirred the syrupy goo.

"Sweet tooth," he said when he caught her gaze.

He downed a long swallow, replaced the cup on the saucer and slid his Ray-Bans down on his nose. There weren't more than a half dozen other people eating breakfast on the terrace. The faint clink of their silverware and the occasional murmured comment barely carried over the sound of the waves hitting the shore. Still, either from habit or instinct, Martin lowered his voice.

"I talked to Rory when I got in last night."

Caro felt her spine stiffen and her smile slip a notch or two. Martin noticed both reactions with a flicker of interest but didn't comment on either.

"Rory says you have everything well in hand."

She relaxed infinitesimally. "I hope so."

"I hope so, too. We hate pulling over a hundred of our operatives out of the field at one time, but the world situation is so volatile right now that we had no choice. They need to know what's going on around them. So we need to make every minute of this conference count."

"You've certainly packed the agenda."

"It's about to get more packed."

Nudging aside his cup, he flipped open his notebook and pulled out a heavily marked-up copy of the schedule. Caro's heart sank at all the insertions and bold black arrows indicating changes.

"Rory and I went over this again last night. He called in some favors and we now have an expert on Africa flying in to brief us on the situation in Zimbabwe. We want to put him on here, right before the update on Tiblesi."

"Okay."

"And we've added two additional SITREPS on the latest developments in Tibet and Venezuela. We can squeeze them in before the live fire demo tomorrow. I'm thinking we'll do one early, during breakfast, and the other at lunch. Make both meals working sessions."

Caro gulped as her meticulously coordinated meal plans fell apart. She'd have to get with the resort's caterer—and *fast*—to make the requested changes. Masking any sign of dismay, she nodded.

"No problem."

"And speaking of the live fire demo…"

Martin flipped to the agreement signed by Captain Antonio Medina, the officer in charge of the *policìa nacional* armory in Girona. Acting as a go-between for GSI and Captain Medina, Caro had put hours into translating, compiling and forwarding the necessary forms. GSI's senior VP of operations now handed her two more.

"See if you can get Medina's chop on these additions to the demo."

"Ice shield?" she read. "Paraclete vest? What are they?"

"The first is a negative energy defense system. We're looking at it for possible deployment to protect high-vis clients when they have to get out among a crowd. The second is a new-generation vest designed to stop armor-piercing bullets. I've tracked down a source here in Spain for both and can have them delivered in time for the demo tomorrow."

He downed a swallow of his syrupy coffee and eyed her over the rims of his Ray-Bans.

"Think you can handle the changes?"

Like she had a choice? Tapping two fingers to her temple, she gave him a brisk salute. "Yes, sir!"

A faint smile softened Martin's chiseled features. "I have to admit I had my doubts when Rory told me he wanted European Business Services, Incorporated, to handle this conference. I didn't think your company had the resources or the experience to pull it together on such short notice. So far, you've proved me wrong."

Caro shifted a little in her seat. She couldn't deny this job would rake in a fat profit for EBS. Still, she resented the way Burke had used it as a pretext to stage a reunion she'd neither anticipated nor wanted.

"Judging by the little exposure I've had to your boss," she said, working hard to keep the acid out of her reply, "I'd say he's used to getting his way."

"Well, he *is* the boss." Martin toyed with his coffee cup and studied her face with a scrutiny that made Caro distinctly uncomfortable. She suspected those cop's eyes saw more than most people wanted them to.

"Rory's a good man," he said after a moment. "The kind you can trust to do what's right."

Depending on your definition of "right," she thought cynically.

"I'll take your word for that."

She glanced at her watch and swallowed another gulp. "Do you have any other items you want to discuss with me?"

"Not right now."

"Then I'd better skip breakfast and get to work on these changes."

"Go."

After dropping off a USB drive with the revised agenda in the business office, Caro met with the resort's conference planner in her den. She, in turn, called in the executive chef.

Andreas was not happy about scratching the second day's elaborate breakfast of fire-grilled Andalucian ham and house specialty *torrijas*. Frowning, he substituted a simpler sausage-and-egg scramble served with flaky rolls and the region's signature apricot jam. He was even less thrilled about changing the elegant seafood lunch buffet planned for outside on the terrace to sit-down service in the ballroom.

Caro left him grumbling over the changes and rushed back to the business office. To her relief, the efficient staff had the revised agendas rolling off the high-speed printer and promised to place them on the tables for the kickoff session.

Those two tasks well in hand, Caro tried to reach Captain Medina. As she'd discovered in her previous dealings with the police captain, he tended to set his own schedule. Luckily, she caught him this time and extracted his promise to review the forms she'd faxed over.

"I need your reply as soon as possible," she begged in the Spanish she'd studied in high school and college. She was almost as fluent in it as in the German she'd mastered during her year in Salzburg with Devon and Sabrina. *"Por favor, capitán."*

"Sí, sí, le llamaré."

Forced to be content with his promise to call, she headed for the ballroom to make sure everything was set for the general session. To her relief, the audiovisual technicians had their equipment up and running. She also confirmed there was plenty of coffee, tea, water and soft drinks available for the attendees who were starting to trickle in. Snatches of conversation caught her ear as she made a last check of the seating arrangements.

"Ramieriz, you old bastard!"

A brawny redhead in a safari shirt with at least a dozen pockets punched the arm of a bearded Latino.

"Heard you got snakebit on that job down in Panama."

They were joined by a slender Asian in a dragon-red dress slit on one side. A head shorter than the two men, she got their instant respect and an eager demand for the details on the Yang Su kidnapping.

Caro ducked out of the ballroom and into the ladies' room to check her hair and lip gloss. Then she drew in a deep breath, pasted on a smile and re-entered the ballroom.

It had filled considerably in her brief absence. Those present were predominantly male, although she picked out several of the dozen or so women slated to attend. Rory was easily identifiable as he moved among the crowd. He'd dressed for the kickoff session in loafers, black slacks and a pale yellow oxford shirt open at the collar. Caro watched from the corner of one eye while he shook hands and thumped backs in that age-old male ritual.

At least one of Rory's crew got a kiss instead of a back thump. Or more correctly, she kissed him. On the cheek, although it was obvious to Caro that the tall, striking blonde would have preferred a full-frontal lip-lock.

For reasons she didn't have time to analyze, Caro formed an instant dislike for the woman. That lasted only until Rory caught sight of his conference coordinator and brought the blonde over for an introduction.

"I want you to meet Sondra Jennings. She's head of GSI's European division, based in Copenhagen. Sondra, this is Caroline Walters, with European Business Services."

The blonde returned Caro's handshake with a friendly smile. "So you're the one who pulled this confab together. Harry Martin was talking about you when we had coffee together a little while ago." Her blue eyes twinkled. "Knowing Harry, I'm sure he's kept you hopping."

"Pretty much," Caro admitted.

"I've worked with several clients who might be interested in the type of services EBS provides. I'll contact them when I get back to Denmark and spread the word."

"That's very generous of you."

"We girls gotta stick together." Her gaze snagged on the man just entering the ballroom. "There's Abdul-Hamid! I haven't seen him since we tracked the source of those death threats against the author of *Inside the Mujahideen.* 'Scuse me, you two."

She hurried to the door and enveloped the newcomer in a monster hug. He returned it with such obvious delight that Caro was forced to revise her initial impression.

"She's very gregarious."

"When she wants to be," Rory drawled. "Ready to get this show under way?"

She swept a final glance over the tables and now-milling crowd. "I am if you are."

"Let's do it."

"I'll be at the back of the room. Just signal if you need anything."

"That won't work." Shaking his head, he caught her elbow and steered her toward a round table near the podium. "I want you up front, with me."

"But…"

"It'll be easier for us to communicate this way."

After seating her beside Harry Martin, he pinned the mobile mike to his shirt. His voice boomed through the speakers.

"All right, team. Time to get to work."

He waited for the general shuffle of chairs to die down before asking Caroline to stand.

"For those of you who haven't met her yet, this is Caroline Walters. She and Harry are running this show. Any complaints, tell him. Any and all kudos go to her."

Rory held the stage for the next hour. Caroline listened in mounting amazement as he discussed worldwide trends in violence against VIPs, quoting specific facts and figures without once referring to the prepared script. It was obvious even to an out-

sider like her that he had every facet of his dangerous profession down cold.

His message was grim, and the slides that flashed
up on the screen were appalling. They depicted, in
graphic detail, a blindfolded French ambassador with
a gun barrel to his head. The bullet-riddled body of
a candidate for prime minister in Indonesia. The terrified wife of a police captain in Colombia, explo-
sives strapped to her chest, just seconds before drug
runners blew her apart as a message to everyone who
cooperated with law enforcement officials.

Caroline was ready for a break by the time Rory
finished. *More* than ready. She didn't view the world
through rose-colored glasses by any means, but
Rory's grim assessment had brought home just how
dangerous it could be.

Particularly for the kind of high-powered executives her company catered to. Neither she nor Devon
nor Sabrina had fully considered that aspect of their
business. The realization sobered Caro and made her
anxious to impart some of this information to her
partners.

"We'll take a short break so they can set up for
lunch," Rory told his people. "Harry will go over the
latest State Department alerts while we eat."

With palpable relief, Caro signaled the servers to
bring in the paella extravaganza she'd arranged for the
kickoff luncheon. Most of the ingredients had been
precooked in the resort's kitchen, but four chefs in tall

white hats provided the finishing touch. Positioned before waist-high stands supporting huge black frying pans, they sizzled the rice, chopped vegetables and cooked seafood morsels over open flames.

The tantalizing aromas soon drew the attendees back into the ballroom. Caro didn't relax until everyone had filled their plates with heaping servings. At Rory's insistence, she brought her plate back to his table.

"You need to listen to Harry's update on State Department alerts," GSI's chief executive advised. "They could play into your business."

"I was thinking that same thing during your briefing. That was pretty scary information you put out."

"It's a scary world."

Nodding, she speared a morsel of calamari and tuned in to Harry Martin's succinct recap.

The rest of the afternoon passed in a blur of country briefings and individual case rundowns. Caro had to duck out to take a call from Captain Medina. She returned with the welcome news that he'd approved the additions to the live fire demo.

The conferees broke for the day at six o'clock. Dinner was scheduled for seven. Since many of the GSI operatives would be feeling a delayed jet lag, Harry had requested Caro keep the meal short and simple. She'd ordered a selection of *tapas* served in a roped-off section of the bar that gave a magnificent view of the bay, followed by salad and chargrilled kebabs. Dessert was a melt-in-your mouth flan with its top seared to a sugary crunch and drizzled with caramel sauce.

A number of the GSI folks folded their tents immediately after dinner. The rest congregated in groups, exchanging war stories that ranged from the ridiculous to the downright gruesome. Caro tried to move unobtrusively between groups to make sure they had everything they needed, but Sondra Jennings drew her into one enclave, Rory into another. By ten o'clock that evening, the colorful espadrilles pinched her toes and she couldn't *wait* to get them off her feet.

Finally she said good-night and left the last die-hards crammed knee-to-knee around a cocktail table. Rory's gaze followed her as she wound through the lounge. Caro could feel it, and the awareness annoyed her no end.

She'd made a determined effort to keep their past out of her head all day. It wasn't that difficult, given how much Rory had changed. She'd watched a stranger kick off the conference today. Informed, incisive, every inch the boss. She didn't know him, any more than he knew her.

Which didn't explain the prickly feeling between her shoulder blades as she left the bar.

Frowning, Caro stepped out onto the tiled veranda. She fully intended to go up to her room, zing off a quick e-mail to Devon and Sabrina and fall into bed. The full moon hanging over the Mediterranean sabotaged those intentions.

She paused, mesmerized by the path the moon had painted across an incandescent sea. The thought of wading into that liquid silver was too much for someone who'd spent half of her life in landlocked Kansas.

The resort sat only a few short yards from the wide seawall encircling the bay. A quick walk brought her to the stone stairs that led down to the sandy shore. Kicking off the espadrilles, Caroline scooped them up in one hand and crossed the hard-packed sand to the water's edge.

The sea breeze carried a damp chill that made her wish she'd gone back to her room for the colorful Spanish shawl she'd purchased at the same time as the espadrilles. Shivering a little, she curled her toes into the sand. The waves washed out, luring her a little farther, and returned with an unexpected wallop.

"Yikes!"

The water was frigid, far colder than she'd anticipated. And much more powerful. The first wave swirled around her ankles. The second hit before she could retreat and soaked her to her knees.

She leaped backward but couldn't escape the undertow. Like a giant vacuum, it sucked the sand right out from under her bare feet and pulled her in. Thrown off balance, Caro stumbled. She saw the next wave roll toward her and floundered backward for one futile step before she went down with an ignominious splash.

The surf boiled up, soaking her. Salt burned her eyes. Cursing, she let go of the espadrilles and slapped the waves. She made a clumsy attempt to get her feet under her, but the sucking undercurrent had her firmly in its grip.

Great! Perfect! At this rate, she'd wash up on the coast of Libya. Thoroughly disgusted, she dug a heel into the shifting ocean bed beneath her.

She'd just found a toehold when a hand clamped around her wrist. The next second, she was jerked to her feet and landed with a thump against a solid wall of chest.

"Caroline! You okay?"

She flipped strands of wet hair out of her eyes and looked up into Rory's taut face.

"I'm fine. Now."

"I almost had a heart attack when I saw you go under. What the hell were you thinking, wading out this far?"

His grip tightened, anchoring her against the next wave. Frigid seawater swirled around her thighs and floated up the hem of her cotton tunic.

"In answer to your question," she said when the swirl subsided, "I didn't *intend* to wade this far. The undertow got me."

"Jesus!"

Almost as wet as she was, he helped her to the

shallows. His pale yellow shirt was plastered against his chest and shoulders. His drenched khakis molded his thighs.

"You scared the crap out of me, woman." Softening both his tone and his grip, he raked her with a swift once-over. "You sure you're okay?"

"I'm fine. Really."

And mortified, now that the initial scare had passed. Getting dragged up on the beach like a half-drowned harbor seal didn't do a whole lot for Caroline's image as a cool, with-it professional.

"Thanks," she added on a grudging afterthought.

"You're welcome." He grinned at her reluctant gratitude. "Rescuing beautiful women is just one of the many services GSI provides. The charge for this particular service is pretty steep, though."

"Send me an invoice. I'll deduct it from the final amount we bill GSI."

"I have a better idea."

Still grinning, he brushed back a wet strand and hooked it behind her ear. His voice dropped to a teasing, all-too-familiar taunt.

"How about I just take it out in trade?"

The situation was so absurd, his touch so unexpected, that Caro didn't have time to block the sudden onslaught of memories.

In a flash, she was seventeen again, hopelessly infatuated, helplessly captivated. Her heart slammed against her ribs. Her pulse shot off the charts. All she could do was stare up in breathless fascination as Burke curled a knuckle under her chin and tipped her head back.

"This is just the first installment," he warned before he swooped down to cover her mouth with his.

Four

Rory initiated the kiss with a clearly defined set of goals.

He wasn't a perpetually aroused young tiger on the prowl anymore. He could control his appetites, harness his primitive instincts. His intention was simply to show Caroline she could trust him. Now.

Then her mouth opened under his, and his intentions were shot all to hell. She tasted of salt and just a hint of sweet, sugary caramel. Through the wet shield of her clothes, he could feel her breasts, hips and belly against his. The ocean thundered in his ears, or maybe it was the sound of her breathing.

He found her tongue with his, and his world shifted, almost tilting him off his feet. Belatedly,

Rory realized it was the damned sand. The powerful undercurrent was siphoning it out from under him.

He raised his head and allowed himself a brief stab of pleasure at the sight of her. Her hair had straggled free of the tight twist. Water spiked her lashes and made them glisten in the moonlight. Her eyes were huge—and rapidly filling with a welter of emotions that included dismay and unmistakable disgust.

With a chuckle, Rory tried to head off the storm he saw coming. "Sucks you in, doesn't it?"

The double entendre was completely unintentional but not lost on either of them. Her breath hissed out, and he backtracked immediately.

"The sand, I mean. I can feel it giving way. Unless you want to rescue *me*, we'd better head for shore."

The water was only ankle high, but the pull was so insistent that he had to wrap an arm around her waist to help her get to dry land. The moment they gained the beach, she jerked away from him.

He could see her fighting for control, struggling with the raw emotions he saw in her face. Rory expected her to lay into him. Was sure she'd deny that second or two when her mouth opened and her tongue danced with his. To his surprise, she took aim at herself.

"What was I thinking? Why *wasn't* I thinking?"

She sounded so appalled, so dismayed, that he had to suppress a wince.

"I never let myself go like that," she said with a break in her voice. "Never!"

Rory's brows soared. "Are you telling me you don't… That you've never…"

His incredulity snapped her out of her miasma of dismay and disgust.

"Never been with anyone but you?" she finished, her chin angling. "Don't flatter yourself, Burke."

But he *had* been the first. The memory of that night beside the river hit Rory hard, low in his belly, as Caroline raised her chin another inch.

"I don't blame you for that…that bit of idiocy. I blame myself. Trust me. It won't happen again."

The hell it wouldn't. Now that he'd had a taste of her, Rory intended to make some revisions to his op plan. Objectives five and six needed considerable adjustments.

He was reworking them in his mind when Caroline whirled and marched all of two yards up the beach before coming to a dead stop. He heard her gasp and followed her line of sight to a set of lighted, floor-to-ceiling windows.

Well, hell! They were there. Harry. Sondra. Abdul-Hamid. The rest of the crew who'd hung around the bar after dinner. All crowded close to the windows, all watching the scene with avid interest. They'd had ringside seats to the entire episode.

"Oh, no," Caroline moaned, more to herself than to him. "How am I supposed to face them in the morning?"

He didn't even try to tell her it was no big deal.

Rory could take the flak from his frolic in the surf. It would hit Caroline hard, he guessed, and not just because of the professional image she worked so hard to project. The past had left her all too vulnerable to whispers and sidelong glances. He was damned if she would be subject to them again because of him.

"I'll do damage control with my people. You don't have to worry about facing them tomorrow—or any other day."

His flat assurance quelled some of Caro's rioting emotions. He sounded so confident, so matter-of-fact. As if wading into the Mediterranean and getting chest-to-chest with a dripping female was no big deal.

Which it probably wasn't. To him. She, on the other hand, could still taste him on her lips.

They parted just inside the foyer. Caroline punched the button for the elevator and refused to look over her shoulder as Rory peeled off toward the bar. Only after she'd gained the safety of her room did she let loose with the torrent churning up inside her.

"Stupid! Stupid! *STU-PID!*"

She wanted to burst into tears. Pound the sofa pillows. Scream or kick or haul off and slug someone. *Anything* to erase the agonizing embarrassment of the past ten minutes.

She was forced to settle for stalking into the bathroom and yanking her wet sweater over her head. Slinging it at the wall gave her a small measure of satisfaction. The sopping cotton hit the tiles with a loud whap. Her slacks and underwear followed in short order.

She stared at the soggy pile, everything inside her cringing with self-disgust. Everything, that is, except a tiny, rebellious corner of her mind that sparked with a life of its own. A nasty little corner that wanted to relive every second of that kiss, to taste the sizzle, feel the heat.

She hadn't lied to Burke. There *had* been other men. Two, to be exact. The first she'd dated for almost six months before she'd let down the barriers enough to go to bed with him. Unfortunately, the sex hadn't been worth the wait.

Her friend Devon had introduced her to the second. A biologist Dev had met at some Let's Go Green function. Ernie was serious about his work but what made him so endearing was his hopeless addiction to old Dean Martin records and any stray cat that happened across his path.

Caro had wanted to love him. She really had. He was so right for her. So gentle and considerate in bed. *Too* gentle and considerate. Try as she might, she couldn't help comparing Ernie's cautious lovemaking to the wild explosion of delight she'd experienced that night beside the river with Rory.

The same wild delight she'd tasted again tonight.

The thrill of it crouched in that forbidden corner of her mind. The excitement was like a fever, swift and all-consuming, straining to break free of Caro's rigid restraints and fire her blood.

Disgusted all over again, she padded on sandy, seaweedy feet to the walk-in shower and twisted the taps to full blast. Face turned to the pounding spray, she let a frustrated groan rip from deep in her throat.

When in *hell* would she learn!

The next morning, she walked into the room set up for the GSI breakfast with a cool smile and her chin high.

She'd had all night to prepare for the smirks and knowing smiles but soon realized that whatever Rory had said to his people must have sunk in. Other than a sideways glance from the male operative with the red hair and a more speculative one from Sondra, everyone was friendly and polite. Gradually, Caroline relaxed.

She snapped wire-tight again the moment Rory appeared. All she had to do was catch a glimpse of him as he strode in and her stomach went into a fast roll. She turned away before he saw her, swallowing a curse when her china coffee cup rattled on its saucer.

She had herself under control by the time he made his way to her side. Exercising iron will, she refused to let either his smile or the faint, tangy scent of his aftershave get to her.

"Morning."

"Good morning."

"You okay?" he asked quietly.

"Fine."

The clipped response didn't seem to faze him. Or keep his glance from drifting downward toward her lips for a few seconds.

"No aftereffects from your late-night swim?"

"Not a one."

The mocking glint that came into his eyes told her he recognized that for the lie it was. Thankfully, Harry Martin came over before he could challenge her on it.

"I've got that situation brief on Venezuela ready to go, boss."

"Let me grab a cup of coffee, and then we'll get started."

As she had the day before, Caroline tried to hang back so she could oversee the meal service. As *he* had the day before, Rory sabotaged her plans.

"After you, Caroline."

The command was politely worded but definitely a command. She thought about saying no for all of three or four seconds. Then she shrugged and accompanied Rory to their designated table.

After the general session detailing the somewhat scary situation in Venezuela, the attendees broke into smaller groups for regional updates. Sondra took charge of the European sessions. Abdul-Hamid orchestrated a series of briefings dealing with the Middle East and Africa. The Asian expert turned out to be a ruddy-faced Englishman with what Caroline could only describe as a seriously warped sense of humor.

Intrigued by roars of laughter emanating from his session, she slipped into the back of the room in time to hear him describe attempts by pirates to hijack a luxury, oceangoing yacht owned by a GSI client.

"They came in under our radar during the night and got close enough to fire their rocket-propelled grenades. Lucky for us the buggers didn't know how to activate the built-in lock-and-launch radar. Bloody grenades came close enough to tighten my knickers, though."

One of the men in the room gave a loud hoot. "Since when do you wear knickers, Basil?"

"It was merely a figure of speech, old chap. Back to our nocturnal visitors…I sincerely wish I could have seen their faces when we whipped the cover off the M61 mounted in the stern, but it was too bloody dark."

Caroline had no idea what an M61 was, but she gathered from the murmurs of approval that it was a powerful weapon. The speaker confirmed that a moment later with his cheerful claim to have blown the buggers right out of the water.

Amazed all over again by the danger Rory's people apparently faced on a daily basis, she slipped out to check on preparations for lunch and finalize transportation to the *policía nacional* armory in Girona.

She had two buses lined up and waiting when the conferees broke after lunch. A truck loaded with sealed crates idled patiently behind the buses. Two of Rory's men had accompanied the crates from the airport and stayed with them for the short trip to Girona.

Caroline had prepped as best she could for the excursion and knew that the ancient city of Girona had been inhabited in turn by Iberians, Romans, Visigoths, Moors and the armies of Napoleon. It had also served as a major center for Kabbalah studies until the Jews were driven out of Spain in 1492. In recent years, Girona had once again become a center of learning for the Jewish faith.

Following directions faxed by Captain Medina, Caroline directed their small convoy to the police armory on the outskirts of town. Antonio Medina strolled out to meet them on their arrival and greeted Caroline in English heavily flavored by his native Catalan roots.

"Good afternoon, Ms. Walters."

"Good afternoon, Captain. Allow me to introduce Rory Burke, president and CEO of Global Security, Incorporated."

Medina thrust out his hand. "I have heard much of you, Mr. Burke. You took part in the international task force that investigated 3/11, yes?"

"I did."

It took Caroline a few moments to make the connection. Nine-eleven was indelibly ingrained on the consciousness of all Americans. Similar horrific attacks had occurred in Spain on March 11, 2004.

Close to two hundred people had died in coordinated commuter train bombings. Almost two thousand more were injured.

She'd had no idea Rory had been part of the multinational task force investigating the bombings. It certainly hadn't been mentioned in his company profile. Then again, maybe that was the kind of expertise you didn't want the bad guys to know you possessed.

It did explain, however, Captain Medina's patience while Caroline had slogged through the reams of paperwork to permit GSI access to his outdoor firing range.

The range was situated in an open field several kilometers from the armory buildings. Medina invited Rory to ride out with him in his vehicle. The rest of the team followed in the buses. Once on the range, the captain, Rory and Harry Martin conferred with the range supervisor. A sense of unreality gripped Caroline as she listened to them discussing laser-directed small-arms fire, armor-piercing bullets and high-impact detonations while swallows chirped merrily in the trees and the bright Catalonian sun warmed the earth.

The first crack of a high-powered, laser-guided sniper rifle sent the swallows flapping. Caro stood well back from the firing line, her ears shielded by cushioned protectors, and felt her jaw drop when a spotter more than a mile and a half downrange signaled back a direct hit.

Even more astonishing was the so-called ice shield. Caro never did grasp the physics involved. Somehow the device activated an intense negative ion field around the target. The hyperactive ions sucked the velocity from most of the bullets fired at the target from various distances. Enough got through, however, for Rory to admit with a wry grin that the device required further testing before being fielded.

After Harry demonstrated the paraclete vest, the GSI agents took turns at the firing line testing an assortment of handguns and ammo. Caroline had no idea she would be included in the live fire exercise until they took a break and Rory beckoned her forward.

"Ever fired one of these?"

She glanced at the blue-steel subcompact nestled in his palm and shook her head. "Nothing that small. I went quail hunting with my father a few times. His double-barrel shotgun just about knocked me flat."

"Given the high-profile clients your firm caters to, a working knowledge of handguns might come in handy."

"I sincerely hope not!"

"We'll start with the basics," he said, calmly brushing aside her objections. "This is the safety. Always check to make sure it's on before handling your weapon."

Fifteen minutes later, Caroline found herself standing between Sondra and Abdul-Hamid on the firing line, peering through shatterproof goggles at a paper target strung from a wire twenty yards away. A borrowed ball cap blocked the sun's glare. Heavy-duty protectors shielded her ears.

Rory stood directly behind her, his body leaning into hers as he corrected her stance. "Don't square off and face the target like that. You won't get good front-to-back balance. You want to form a pyramid, with your power leg forward."

"Which one is my power leg?"

"You're right-handed. You'll naturally favor your right leg. Now angle your pelvis at forty-five degrees to the target. A little more."

Oh, sure! Like she could think pyramids and angles with his hands on her hips and her rear jammed against the fly of his jeans.

"With an automatic, you want to use what we call a 'crush' grip. The harder you hold the weapon, the less it will kick."

"A tight grip also lessens the chance some sleaze-bag can knock it out of your hand," Sondra volunteered.

Caroline diverted her attention long enough to see that a circle of interested observers had gathered to watch the lesson. Then Rory reached around her to steady her arms, and every nerve in her body snapped back to the task at hand.

"Use your thumb to release the safety. That's it. Now tuck your thumb and focus on the front sight.

You want to pull the trigger straight back. Squeeze it or roll it. Don't jerk it. All set?"

"I think so."

He dropped his arms and stepped back. "Fire when ready."

Her first shot went wide of the target and kicked her arms up. The second wasn't much better. With cordite stinging her nostrils, Caroline scowled, tightened her grip and squinted through the front sight.

The next three shots peppered the edges of the target silhouette. The sixth and seventh hit dead center. Cheers and hoots erupted from the observers as Caro lowered the weapon and engaged the safety.

"You're a natural," Rory said after he'd taken charge of the automatic.

"Beginner's luck."

"Trust me. Not all beginners can find a target."

His smile of approval stayed with Caro all the way back to the resort. She felt it almost as much as the disturbing aftereffects of her close encounter with his zipper.

It took Caroline the rest of the evening and most of the night to comprehend her inexplicable reaction every time Rory got within striking distance. When she padded into the bathroom just before seven the next morning and braced her hands on the marble sink, she had it all figured out.

"It's simple," she told the tangled-haired woman

in the mirror. "The man represents temptation. Danger. Forbidden desire. Everything you've gone out of your way to avoid in the years since high school."

She'd worked so hard to suppress her past. With deliberate intent, she'd chosen a nice, safe profession. Dated nice, safe men. Established a nice, safe routine. Not until she'd gotten together with Sabrina and Devon last year and taken a hard look at her life did Caro realize she'd mortgaged her future to her past.

Quitting her job and joining forces with her friends to launch EBS had been a *major* step in a new direction. Admitting that Rory Burke still turned her on after all these years was another.

"There," she threw at the face in the mirror, "you've acknowledged it. You want his touch."

She wanted more than that. With brutal honesty, she could admit she wanted his mouth and hands and lean, hard body all over hers. The realization shook her right down to her core. It also made her turn to the two friends she'd come to depend on for support and advice.

Whirling, Caro stalked back into the bedroom and flipped up the lid of her laptop. She caught her business partners at their computers, checking morning e-mail. A few clicks later, she had their faces displayed side by side. Devon's hair lit up the laptop's screen in a blaze of dark red. Sabrina raked a hand through her tumble of blond curls and demanded an instant update.

"So what's happening with Burke? Have you hauled off and decked him yet?"

"Not exactly."

"I'm still available to do the job for you. So is Marco, by the way."

"And Cal," Devon put in.

Oh, sure. That's all Caroline needed. Their two bristling males confronting a former Army ranger and all-around tough guy.

"The situation has, uh, changed a little."

"Changed how?"

She tapped a nail on the laptop keyboard. How to explain this insidious heat, this growing hunger, to friends who had watched her put her emotions on total lockdown for so many years?

"The thing is, I'm…er…sort of…attracted to Rory."

Talk about understatements, Caro thought ruefully as the two faces on the laptop screen took on looks of almost identical astonishment. While they were still struggling to recover, she told them about the kiss that followed her dip in the ocean and the itchy feelings that had almost consumed her at the firing range yesterday.

"The conference wraps up tomorrow morning," she said. "Part of me wants to just crawl in a hole until Rory leaves for the airport in the afternoon. But there's this other confused, completely idiotic part that doesn't want him to go."

"Well," Sabrina said after a long silence, "sounds like there's something between you and this guy Burke. Call it unfinished business or chemistry or plain old-fashioned lust, the fact that it revved to life after more than a decade says something."

"I *know!* But what?"

"Beats me. Dev, what do you think?"

Devon pursed her mouth to one side. Like Caro and Sabrina, she'd made her share of mistakes, most notably the brief marriage to her jerk of an ex. She hadn't expected to tumble into love with Cal Logan, EBS's first big client. Dev still pinched herself every day to make sure she wasn't dreaming. Caroline suspected that's why she took her time before slowly replying.

"I think… I think Sabrina may be right. This unexpected reunion has stirred emotions you've tried to repress for years. Maybe you should get them out of your system once and for all. Or more precisely get *Burke* out of your system."

"Are you suggesting what I think you are?"

"Look, you said you're still attracted to him. I suspect in your mind you still see the young stud who fed your adolescent fantasies. The man he is now may not live up to those fantasies, but there's only one way to find out."

"Hot, mindless sex."

"If that's what your instincts are telling you. Go with them, Caro. See where they take you."

"We all know where they took her last time," Sabrina protested.

"She was seventeen and a virgin. She's a lot older this time around."

"Thanks," Caroline drawled.

"You know what I mean."

That was just it. She did.

"One thing is for sure," she vowed. "Whatever happens between Rory and me will *not* include unprotected sex. I'm still on the pill, thank God."

She'd never gone off it after nice, safe Ernie. Even then she'd insisted they use condoms. Nothing like a healthy dose of paranoia to flavor a relationship.

"So," Sabrina mused, "the real question is whether whatever happens between you and Burke will include *any* kind of sex."

Caro blew out a sigh. "At this point, your guess is as good as mine."

Five

Rory initiated the next phase of Operation Caroline Walters early on the third day of the conference.

This particular objective required that he get her alone. Away from all distractions. Out from under the curious eyes of his people. He'd planned a private dinner in his suite to "discuss" conference business, but the phone call he received that morning from a potential client in Barcelona provided a much better target of opportunity.

Snapping his cell phone shut, he went looking for Caroline and Harry Martin. He found them together, conferring over yet another addition to the schedule. The kick to his gut when he noted the silky tendril that had escaped her neat twist and curled at her nape resolved any doubts about his course of action.

Harry looked up at his approach and sensed instantly that something was up. The man knew him too well, Rory thought wryly.

"Hey, boss. Need something?"

"Yeah, I do. Check out a guy named Juan Casteel for me. He owns a shipping company based in Barcelona."

"Juan Casteel." He jotted down the name. "What's his angle?"

"He says he needs more protection."

"Who doesn't?" Harry muttered.

"Casteel found out I'm in Spain and wants to meet with me. I've set up an appointment at his office for three this afternoon."

"I'll get on him."

"Caroline, I need you to go with me. Casteel's English is pretty heavily accented. I'd like a second set of ears to make sure I understand him."

Rory ignored the quick glance Harry shot his way. "Pack an overnight bag," he instructed his surprised conference coordinator. "Casteel said something about dinner at his place, so I could meet his wife and see the layout of his house. If they eat as late as most Spaniards, it'll be too late to drive back tonight."

Dinner or no dinner, Rory had already determined he and Caroline would *not* hit the road again tonight.

"Better make hotel reservations," he told her. "We'll take my rental car. I'll meet you in the lobby at noon."

She waffled, clearly uncertain and wary. He didn't give her time to recover.

"Let me know what you dig up on Casteel, Harry."

His deputy gave him a hard look before nodding. "Will do."

Harry delivered a background dossier on Juan Casteel to Rory's suite forty-five minutes later. The Spanish shipping magnate didn't top the list of his priorities, however.

"Let's have it, boss. What the hell are you up to with Caroline?"

Rory paused in the act of stuffing his shaving kit into his carryall. "What makes you think I'm up to anything?"

"Don't give me that bull. I'm the one who kept your ass out of jail, remember?"

"How could I forget? You remind me at least once a month."

Never one to mince words, the retired cop set his jaw. "Caroline's a good kid, but she's not in your league. You hurt her again, and you'll answer to me."

"Again?" Rory echoed softly.

"You think I'm getting senile or something?"

Disgusted, Harry tossed the background dossier to the bed beside the leather carryall.

"I knew there had to be some reason behind your insistence that her company handle this conference. I did a little digging. Didn't take long to figure out you were the one who knocked her up."

Wincing at the blunt assessment, Rory yanked on the zipper of his carryall. "Does it make any difference that I didn't *know* I'd knocked her up?"

"Not to me. Or to her, I suspect. What's your game?"

"It's no game, Harry. I intend to atone for past sins."

"How?"

He couldn't lie to the man who'd become his conscience. "My first plan was a cash settlement. I know money wouldn't make up for what she went through, but it could ease the future for her. If she wouldn't accept it outright, I planned to disguise it by steering business her way. Now…"

Now all he could think of was how Caroline had looked in the moonlight. How she'd tasted, so warm and salty. How much he wanted to taste her again.

"I'm thinking maybe a more permanent arrangement."

"Like marriage?"

"Maybe."

"Little late for that, isn't it?"

"Better late than never. Besides, we both know I would have made a rotten husband back then. I was too young and too much of a wiseass."

"You won't get any argument from me on that. I'm curious, though. Why do you think you'll make a better husband now? You haven't spent more than a few weeks in that empty barn you call home in the past year. Then there's the little matter of your line of work."

With a jerk of his chin, Harry indicated the scars webbing the back of Rory's hand.

"Think you can bust in car windows and haul clients out of burning vehicles indefinitely?"

"Yeah, well, that's part of my rationale."

Rory glanced down and made a fist. He hadn't been able to perform that simple act for months after the job in Seattle went sour.

"We both know the odds, Harry. The higher the profile of our clients, the greater the chances we'll take a hit along with them. Conversely, the greater the risk, the greater the reward. I've got more money in the bank than I can spend in two lifetimes."

"And no one to leave it to," his longtime friend and mentor guessed shrewdly, "except the half dozen charities that hit you up on a regular basis. So you're going to make Caroline a rich widow."

"Not anytime soon, hopefully. But one way or another, she'll be set for life."

"Just out of curiosity," Harry said, "what makes you so sure Caroline will have you?"

"I'm not sure at all. But there's something between us that just won't die. A spark. A flame. Whatever. It's been smoldering all these years."

"Yeah, I noticed you out there on the beach the

other night, fanning the fire." He palmed his salt-and-pepper buzz cut and eyed Rory thoughtfully. "Have you told her about your plans for her future?"

"Not yet."

"When are you planning to spring them on her?"

"I'm not sure. Tonight, maybe, in Barcelona."

Harry nodded once, slowly. "I repeat, kid. Hurt that girl again and you'll answer to me."

"Understood. Now give me a quick recap of what you dug up on this guy Casteel."

Caroline decided the meeting with Rory's high-powered prospective client required more professional attire than the semicasual outfits she'd worn at the conference. She changed into black pumps, her slim black skirt with its matching jacket worn over an aqua silk tank.

She was glad she'd made the switch when Rory met her in the lobby. He, too, had changed and was once again the consummate executive in a hand-tailored charcoal-gray suit and silk tie. He looked almost like a stranger again until his amber eyes met hers and a frisson of unsettling sensation rippled down her spine.

"Ready?"

At her nod, he took her overnight bag and carried it with his to the silver BMW waiting at the front entrance. The smiling valet opened the door for her. It closed with a well-mannered thud, shutting her and

Rory in a cage of cloud-soft leather and high-performance engineering.

Caroline said little during the drive into the city. As they sped along the A7 *Autopista,* snippets from her early-morning colloquy with Devon and Sabrina kept replaying inside her head.

Time's running out.

Do I go with my instincts or play it smart and safe this time?

Her fingers tightened on the directions Señor Casteel had provided to his downtown office. She slanted a glance at the man beside her and found only traces of the teenager she'd hungered for in his rugged profile.

This Rory Burke was so different and so dangerously compelling. The square chin, the crinkles at the corners of his eyes, the nose with the flattened bridge—each of the parts added up to a whole that made Caroline's adolescent desire pale by comparison to the hunger he roused in her now.

It hit her again, a hot rush of desire that made her belly clench and anticipation whip through her like wildfire. They had tonight, she thought. Alone. In a city made for lovers.

Go with your instincts.

See where they take you.

He turned then and met her gaze. Those wolf's eyes seemed to burn right through her. "Is this it?"

"Wh-What?"

"C-33." He tipped his head toward the green highway sign flashing by. "Isn't this where we cut off?"

"Oh. Right. C-33."

Jerked back to her self-appointed navigator duties, Caroline consulted the handwritten directions. Barcelona's sprawling suburbs soon engulfed them, with accompanying traffic and noise.

"C-33 turns into Avenue Meridiana about a mile ahead. We stay on that until we hit Avenue Diagonal." A brown sign snagged her attention. "The Diagonal takes us right past the Sagrada Familia."

"The what?"

"The Sagrada Familia, Barcelona's famous unfinished cathedral. It's one of Antoni Gaudí's masterpieces, along with La Pedrera and Casa Batlló."

She clicked her tongue at his blank look.

"You said you've visited Barcelona twice before. Didn't you see any of Gaudí's work?"

"Not unless he built the bar where I spent the better part of a three-day pass." His grin was quick and unrepentant. "I was still in the Army then. The next time I hit the city, I was on business. Landed at noon, left at seven that night. No time for sightseeing."

"What a shame. Barcelona holds some of the world's greatest architectural treasures. Maybe we can squeeze in a side trip or two while we're here."

"Maybe," he agreed with a look she couldn't quite interpret. "Looks like we're coming up on Avenue Meridiana."

In Caroline's considered opinion, Barcelona was a world-class mecca for art lovers of all persuasions. On previous trips she'd spent hours in the Picasso Museum. One whole afternoon was occupied by wandering Montjuic, site of the 1929 World's Fair and now filled with the wild and wonderful sculptures by Spain's great Joan Miró. But Gaudí's unfinished cathedral had truly left an indelible imprint on her.

Its towers appeared in the distance soon after they turned onto Avenue Diagonal, spearing into the blue sky with the soaring power of the apostles they were intended to represent. Eight additional towers were still under construction. Huge cranes had been an integral feature of the cathedral landscape since its foundation was laid in 1882.

Vowing to get Rory in for a closer look, Caroline directed him down Avenue Diagonal, then onto the city's fashionable north-south artery, Paseo de Gracia.

"There's the fountain Señor Casteel said to look for." She pointed to the five-tiered sculpture shooting jets of silvery water high into the air. "His office building should be on the next block."

Following the directions, Rory turned into an underground parking lot and pulled into the spot that had been reserved for him next to the elevators. Moments later, he ushered Caroline into an eighth-floor corridor flooded with light and stopped dead.

"What the hell is that? A giant chess set?"

She followed his startled gaze to the window at the end of the corridor. The sparkling glass gave a clear view of the rooftop of the building across the street.

"Those are chimneys and air vents!"

Thrilled, Caroline dragged him to the window for a closer look at the dozens of fanciful figures sprouting from the wavy roof. Below the modernistic sculptures was an art-deco-style apartment complex decorated with undulating wrought-iron balconies.

"That's La Pedrera. A series of residences Gaudí designed for the Mila family in the early 1900s. He described the roof sculptures as sentinels in the sky."

"Weird," Rory muttered, fascinated despite himself.

"Ha! If you think those are weird, wait until you see his Casa Batlló. The balconies all look like skulls."

"And you like this kind of architecture?"

"I love it."

"No accounting for tastes," he said with one of his quicksilver grins.

Caroline knew then she was in trouble. *Major* trouble. All the man had to do was flash that killer grin and she went gooey inside.

Just like last time, a voice in her head shouted. All those years ago. When he'd glance up, catch her watching him. One corner of his mouth would lift in a sardonic, knowing smile, and she would fall apart.

She'd ached for him then with a schoolgirl's passion. There wasn't anything the least girlish about the desire that now tightened Caroline's nipples under the silk tank top and stirred a damp heat between her thighs.

Some of that wild hunger must have shown in her face. Rory's smile lost its cocky tilt. The tanned skin stretched tight across his cheeks. He leaned in, his gaze holding hers, and brushed a knuckle over her cheek.

"Let's go take care of business. All of a sudden I've got an uncontrollable urge to see more of this guy Gaudí's crazy architecture."

Architecture was the *last* thing on Rory's mind as he escorted Caroline up the steps of Juan Casteel's palatial town house later that evening.

He'd spent a good four hours in the shipping magnate's office, pumping him for precise details regarding his business, his lifestyle, his current security arrangements and the threats that had prompted him to consider additional expertise.

Now, with the night breeze stirring the soft tendrils that had escaped Caroline's smooth twist and her scent teasing his nostrils, he was seriously regretting that he'd agreed to mix business with pleasure for another few hours.

He shoved aside the regret to note with approval the two cameras that screened visitors from separate angles. After he and Caroline complied with a polite request to hold their IDs up to cameras, a uniformed maid opened the door. She showed them into a three-story foyer dominated by a massive stained-glass chandelier.

"Ah, you're right on time."

Juan Casteel and his wife came down a sweeping circular staircase to greet them. He was a big man in his late sixties, with a loud voice and gnarled hands left over from his early years on the docks. By contrast, his wife was slim and elegant and wore her age with great dignity.

"This is my bride of forty years," Casteel boomed, beaming with pride. "To this day, I don't know why she married a great oaf like me."

"I wonder that myself sometimes," she teased in flawless English as she held out a hand. "You must be Ms. Walters. I'm so glad you and Mr. Burke could join us."

"Please, call me Caroline."

"With pleasure. And I am Elena."

While Señora Casteel entertained Caroline over cocktails, her husband gave Rory a tour of their magnificent home. Built in the 1890s, it was opulently decorated and well guarded. Dinner afterward was a protracted affair in the best Spanish style, with a half dozen courses and fine wines.

As the evening drew to a close, Rory waged a fierce internal debate over the best way to initiate the next phase of his plan. He had several options lined up when he and Caroline checked into the five-star Hotel Grand Royale. She'd reserved separate rooms—a suite for him, more modest accommodations for her.

Not that she'd need them. When Rory keyed the lock to his suite, he'd narrowed his options to two. Neither involved separate beds.

His careful planning proved completely unnecessary the moment he ushered Caroline inside. To his sardonic amusement, this character Gaudí had set the perfect seduction scene.

There it was, the architect's unfinished cathedral, bathed in golden light and perfectly framed in the sliding glass doors leading to the terrace.

"Ooooooh!"

Enraptured, Caroline headed straight for the doors. Rory dropped their bags on the suite's antique rolled-arm sofa and followed. A cold, damp breeze swirled across the terrace, but Caroline didn't seem to notice as she laid both palms on the wide balustrade and drank in the view. Rory positioned himself behind her and slightly to one side, blocking the worst of the wind.

He had to admit the cathedral made an impressive sight as it soared above the city lights. The magnificent structure couldn't compare with Caroline Walters, however. With the reflected glow illuminating her profile and the wind tugging a few strands from the twist at the back of her head, she ignited a slow burn in Rory's belly.

He savored the heat and the sight of her for a few

moments before reaching out to release the clip holding her hair. The rest of her golden-brown mane spilled loose and brought her head turning toward him in surprise.

"I've been wanting to do that for the past four days," he told her, sliding his hand under the silky tangle.

He gave her plenty of warning. More than enough time to pull away. The fact that she didn't was like a hard, swift punch to his gut.

"I've been wanting to do this, too," he muttered, "ever since our little stroll in the surf."

Slowly, inexorably, he drew her closer. Just as slowly, he angled his head. He'd swooped in the other night and caught her off guard. This time he wanted her fully aware and quivering with anticipation.

In almost the next breath, he questioned his plan. One brush of his mouth over hers and every tendon in his body went wire-tight. One taste and he had to fight the fierce urge to devour her.

Then she drew back, looked up with wide, solemn eyes and proceeded to shock the hell out of him.

"I think we should have sex."

Six

Even before Rory recovered from his stunned surprise, he'd formulated two possible responses to the blunt suggestion. He could ask Caroline what had prompted it. Or he could act now and ask later.

He'd always preferred action to words.

In one swift move, he had her in his arms. A moment later he was striding through the living room. Soft lamplight showed the way to a bedroom that might have been designed for just the kind of activities Rory had in mind.

Elegant antiques and lush fabrics gave the room a rich, seductive feel. The king-size sleigh bed had already been turned down. Gold-wrapped Godiva chocolates rested on the mounded pillows while blue bottles of Perrier and a split of French champagne occupied a tray on one nightstand.

Several erotic uses for the chocolates and champagne leaped instantly into his head. Later, he told himself sternly. Much later. Right now his most pressing task was to get Caroline out of her clothes before she started having second or third thoughts.

He eased his arm from under her knees and let her slide to her feet. The friction that generated got him instantly hard. Tight and aching below his belt, he buried a hand in her hair and covered her mouth with his.

She hesitated just long enough to nearly give Rory heart failure before she locked her arms around his neck. To his profound relief, her mouth was as hungry as his, her tongue every bit as eager.

The taste of her went straight to his bloodstream, as powerful and as potent as a shot of whiskey. Mere seconds later he had her suit jacket unbuttoned and the silky top peeled off to reveal a lacy half bra in a pale shade of blue.

Curling a knuckle, he drew it down the slope of her breast, then slid his hand under the soft contour. His thumb flicked the dusky tip just visible through the lace. The nipple budded almost instantly.

He played with it, brushing his thumb back and forth until her breath rasped. Then he turned his attention to her other breast. Supported by his arm, she leaned back to give him freer access. Rory took full advantage of her vulnerable position to bend and nip at her tender flesh.

Palming his hand along the curve of her waist, he tugged down her skirt zipper. The black fabric pooled around her pumps. He wasn't sure what he'd expected to find underneath. The frivolous garter belt almost drove him over the edge right then and there. He couldn't believe it when he heard himself ask, "You sure you want to do this?"

Cheeks flushed, her green eyes bright with desire, she nodded. "I'm sure."

Caroline thought she knew what to expect. The only other time Rory had peeled off her clothes and used his hands and tongue on her, he'd had her writhing and gasping and groaning within moments. The sharp ache when he'd penetrated had generated more surprise than pain. Awkward and untutored, she'd followed his gruff instructions until nature took over and she was thrusting her hips up to meet his.

She'd gained more expertise in the years since. But none of it prepared her for the animal lust that grabbed her by the throat when Rory stretched her out on the bed, unsnapped her garters and slowly, so slowly, rolled down her nylons.

His eyes were as hot as his hands when he stood to strip off his own clothes. Yanking at his tie, he swept his gaze from her breasts to her ankles.

"God, you're beautiful."

Caroline's first instinct was to drag the duvet over and shield herself. Her brief spurt of embarrassment lasted only until Rory's suit coat, tie and dress shirt came off to reveal a chest corded with lean, hard muscle.

"So are you," she gasped as her belly went tight.

He grinned at the compliment. "Please don't repeat that in front of Harry. Or any of my people. Doesn't go with my tough-guy image."

What *did* go with the image were the scars crisscrossing the back of his left hand. Breathing hard, Caroline zeroed in on the faint white web while he unbuckled his belt and tugged down his zipper.

When he shucked his slacks and shorts, she forgot the scars, forgot her thumping heart, almost forgot how to breathe. His jutting erection reminded her that she'd never seen him naked. Neither of them had shed all their clothing that night at the river. She'd been too shy; he'd been too eager. And God knew neither of the two men she'd allowed into her bed since then had looked anything like this!

Yielding to an urge she didn't even try to control, she scrambled awkwardly to her knees and wrapped her hand around his rigid flesh. Rory jerked, obviously surprised by the move. Caroline was almost as surprised as him at her uncharacteristic boldness but wasn't about to back off now.

Tightening her fist, she slid it down, then up again. The semiloose cowl near the tip disappeared. Veins popped out under the hot, velvety skin. Reveling in an incredible sense of power, she cupped his sac with her other hand. When a bead of clear liquid appeared on the tip of his shaft, she conquered the last of her inhibitions and leaned forward to lick it.

"Uhhh. Salty."

Her involuntary grimace earned a laugh from Rory. The next moment she was flat on her back. His weight pinned her to the fluffy duvet. His knee pried hers apart.

"My turn."

Spreading her legs, he slid his hand down her belly and between her thighs. His fingers combed the curls covering her mound. His thumb found the hypersensitive nub at her center. She was practically gushing all over his hand when he nudged her a little farther up on the bed.

The rasp of his tongue against her clit arched her spine. The subsequent sucking almost levitated her off the mattress. Mere seconds later, she climaxed in a white-hot flash of pure sensation.

She rode the crashing waves for moments. Maybe hours. Finally the ceiling stopped spinning, the exquisite sensations subsided and mortification set in.

"I'm so sorry! I didn't mean for it to end that quickly. You haven't… I didn't…"

"No apologies necessary."

A wicked glint came into his eyes as he rolled off the bed and fished a condom out of his wallet.

"We're not done. In fact, Ms. Walters, the night has just begun."

He ripped the foil package open with strong white teeth. Caroline didn't tell him she was taking birth-control pills. The more protection, she thought as heat began to swirl in her belly again, the better.

Rory proved as good as his word. They weren't done. Not by any measure in the book.

Caroline couldn't quite believe her hedonistic responses to his lovemaking. Then again, he was so incredibly good at it. He entered her slowly, stretching her, filling her, and withdrew just as slowly.

The next thrust was harder and faster.

Then slow again.

He soon had her almost weeping with pleasure, but she was determined to take him with her this time. Panting, she used every bit of her strength to squeeze her vaginal muscles. His grunt gave her a fierce, almost primal, satisfaction. So did the fists he buried in her hair to anchor her for another series of swift, hard thrusts that—finally!—sent them both over the edge.

As the last sensations from that unbelievable session drained away, Rory curled her into his side. Together, they sank into total oblivion.

When Caroline resurfaced, sunlight slanted through the crack in the drawn curtains, and a heavy weight encircled her waist.

The weight was an arm, she discovered after a tentative exploration. She ran a hand over its dusting of gold fuzz while her sleepy haze slowly evaporated.

"'Bout time you woke up," a husky voice whispered into her ear.

Her mouth tasted like moldy cheese, and she had to pee in the worst way...until Rory tightened his arm and drew her into the cradle of his hips. He was primed and already poking at her bare bottom. When his hand moved to her breast and teased her nipple into an aching peak, an involuntary slickness overlaid the sticky residue on her thighs.

He wedged a knee between hers and opened her. When he slid in, she was wet and ready.

Afterward, Caroline still had to pee but couldn't summon enough energy to roll out of bed. She lay limp and totally boneless, with just enough strength left to stroke his arm and the hand still cupping her breast.

His skin was tanned and dark against hers. Idly, she drew a nail over his wrist and traced the faint white scars on the back of his hand.

"How did you get these?"

"Busting in the window of a burning limo. My client was trapped inside."

He said it with such lazy indifference. As if dragging a client from a blazing limousine constituted an everyday occurrence.

Maybe it did. After sitting in on some of the

conference briefings, Caroline had gained an out-sider's appreciation of the risks Rory and his people faced every day.

"Now I have a question for you," he said, inter-rupting her uneasy thoughts.

He rested his chin on the top of her head. His breath tickled her ear as he hitched her a little higher in the cradle of his thighs.

"What made you decide we should have sex? Not that I'm complaining, mind you. In fact, I'd already decided we wouldn't need the second room."

"Is that so?"

"Yeah, babe, it is. But I have to say you shocked the hell out of me with your cool pronouncement."

"That was the intent."

"I figured. What I can't figure, is why you decided not to fight whatever this is between us."

"I'll tell you. But first I have to hit the bathroom."

Rory loosened his hold enough to let her scoot to her side of the bed. She dragged the lightweight duvet with her. Its ends trailed after her as she re-treated to a cavern of cool marble and gold-plated fixtures.

She traded the duvet for one of the thick terry-cloth robes hanging from padded hangers on the back of the bathroom door. She would have loved a shower but had to make do with a washcloth and the hotel's scented soap. The basket of goodies on the mile-long vanity also included complimentary toothbrushes, thank God! After finger-combing her tangled hair, Caroline faced her nemesis once more.

He was relaxed against the padded headboard. A tangled sheet pooled at his waist, baring his flat belly. Golden bristles stubbled his cheeks and chin, and his hair stood up in short, disordered spikes.

"I called room service," he informed her. "Coffee and hot rolls are on the way."

He patted the mattress in an unmistakable invitation for breakfast in bed. Caroline shoved her hands in the pockets of the robe and stayed where she was.

"You asked why I decided to sleep with you. It's simple."

"To you, maybe."

"I thought I'd wiped you out of my head years ago. Seeing you again so unexpectedly brought back all the confusion, all the unfinished business. I decided to stop fighting the emotions you rouse and work through them instead. The idea is to get you out of my system once and for all."

Lifting a brow, he regarded her with lazy amusement. "Did it work?"

"I don't know. Too early to tell."

She was lying through her teeth. She knew it. He knew it. Everything in her ached to slide back between the rumpled sheets. Instead, she glanced pointedly at the clock on the antique nightstand.

"It's almost eight. The conference wrap-up is scheduled for eleven."

After which he'd fly back to California, and his people would disperse to the four corners of the globe. Caro would stay over until tomorrow to take care of last-minute details, then fly to Virginia. They'd have a continent between them. The prospect closed her throat even as Rory leered and patted the sheet.

"We'd better hustle, then. Come here, woman."

"We can't. Not again. We'll barely make it back to Tossa in time as it is."

He gave in eventually and scooped up his clothes. As he padded to the bathroom, Caroline assured herself she'd done exactly the right thing.

She'd followed her gut instincts. Spent a wild night in his arms. Now she needed to step back. Let time and distance bring the closure she hadn't known she needed.

A little less than an hour later, they had both showered, dressed and consumed the breakfast Rory had added to the room service order.

"We should beat the morning rush hour," he commented as they took the elevator to the lobby. "We'll be heading out of the city, against the traffic."

The lobby was an explosion of lush palms, marble pillars and gleaming, gold-plated fixtures. Interspersed among the palms were boutiques bearing names such as Cartier and Antonio Miró.

Caroline refused to feel guilty when Rory handed in both keys and signed the tab. It wasn't her fault

GSI would get stuck with the tab for an unused room. Not completely, anyway.

"I called down for my car."

"Yes, Mr. Burke. The valet has it waiting for you at the front entrance."

"Thanks."

The casual hand Rory placed at the small of Caroline's back burned right through her suit jacket and silk top. She felt its heat as they recrossed the lobby and made for the silver BMW parked outside the old-fashioned revolving doors.

They were almost at the entrance when a colorful display in the window of the hotel's exclusive flower shop snagged his attention. Pausing, he eyed the ruby-red crystals suspended by silver ribbons to form a large, sparkling heart. A massive bouquet of red roses blossomed in the center of the heart.

"What's the date today?" he asked Caroline.

"The fourteenth."

"Valentine's Day." He grinned. "Appropriate, wouldn't you say?"

Appropriate for what? A night of erotic sex, after which they would each go their separate ways? Somehow that scenario didn't say hearts and flowers to Caro. As she tried to point out when Rory suggested she wait for him in the car.

"The occasion doesn't call for romantic gestures. You don't need to buy me roses. Besides, we don't have time for that now."

"I won't be long," he assured her.

Okay, so maybe she would take a single long-stemmed rose home with her and press it between the pages of a book. When she took it out years from now, she could finger its dry, brittle petals and remember her second walk on the wild side.

And this time a rose was *all* she'd take home with her.

Relieved and a just a little depressed by the thought, Caroline shrugged and pushed through the revolving doors.

She was chewing on her lower lip and taking a third look at her watch when Rory finally joined her, sans roses.

"Couldn't find what you wanted?"

"Actually, I found *exactly* what I wanted." He keyed the ignition and teased her with a smile. "I thought I'd wait and give it to you later, over dinner."

"Dinner? But I thought you were flying home this afternoon, right after the conference."

"I was. I changed my reservation."

"When?"

"Yesterday, when I found out you were staying over until tomorrow."

She slumped back against the seat, too surprised to comment while he maneuvered into the city traffic. He waited until they were headed north on the wide Avenue Diagonal to shoot her a quizzical glance.

"Did you think I was going to just pack up and leave you here in Spain?"

"Why would I think anything else?"

He grimaced and cut the wheel to move into the left lane. "I suppose I deserved that. But I'm not hopping on a motorcycle—or an MD-80 jumbo jet— and roaring out of town. Not this time, Caroline."

She frowned, trying to get a handle on his motives. Even more difficult to grasp was her own inexplicable reaction to the fact they'd have another night together.

"What makes this time any different from the last?"

"We'll talk about that tonight," he promised. "At dinner."

Thrown for a complete loop, she had no choice but to sit back and count the mileposts on the *Autopista* until they approached the exit for Tossa de Mar.

Seven

They made it back to the resort with barely enough time to change before the wrap-up session.

Caroline raced up to her own room and scrambled into a black ankle-length crinkle skirt and her wide-sleeved tangerine tunic. She had started to clip her hair up in its usual neat twist when she spotted a red mark on her neck.

Well! Looks like she'd acquired a souvenir from her second walk on the wild side after all. A perfect match with the unfamiliar ache in her thighs. That's what she got for overworking muscles that hadn't been exercised in years. Grimacing, she left the dark, heavy mass down and swirling around her shoulders.

The first person she saw when she went downstairs again was Sondra Jennings. The blonde had already checked out of her room and was wheeling her suitcase down the hall toward the conference center.

"Hey, Caroline. We missed you at dinner last night."

"I drove into Barcelona with Rory."

"Yeah, I heard." The wheels rattled over the undulating terra-cotta tiles as she gave Caro a considering glance. "Listen, you can tell me to butt out if you want. There's something you should know, though. If you don't already."

Caroline guessed what was coming and cringed inside. Talk about history repeating itself! One night with Rory and already she was the recipient of knowing glances. Would the smirks and snickers come next?

"What?" she asked with a touch of ice.

"Rory's one of the good guys. The kind you want watching your back. And if you let him," she added with a waggle of her delicately penciled brows, "he'll do a pretty good job of watching the front, too."

Her roguish expression melted Caroline's reserve. Relaxing, she returned the blonde's smile.

"I'll keep that in mind. But you've got it wrong, Sondra. Rory and I had some unfinished business to take care of. That's all."

"Yeah. Uh-huh. Sure. You keep telling yourself that."

The suitcase bumped along for a few more tiles.

"I know him, Caroline. He doesn't go into any

situation blind. He knows exactly what his objective is and how best to achieve it."

No kidding! Rory had made it clear his objective in this particular situation had been to right an old wrong. *Her* objective last night had been to exorcise the sexual pull he exerted on her once and for all. So much for either of them accomplishing what they'd set out to.

"And there's the one whereof we speak," Sondra murmured, tipping her chin toward the man striding toward them from the opposite end of the hall.

He, too, had changed out of the clothes he'd worn for his meeting with Juan Casteel. The suit and tie were gone, replaced by dark slacks and a red polo shirt embroidered with the GSI logo. His smile gave only the barest hint of the hours they'd spent exchanging bodily fluids last night and this morning.

"Harry needs to talk to you," he told Caroline. "He has a question about the exit permits for weapons we brought in."

"Where is he?"

"He was heading for the business office when I left him a few moments ago."

"I'll go track him down. Sondra, I know you have to leave before the wrap-up ends. I've scheduled a car for eleven-thirty. It'll be waiting for you."

"Thanks."

"Have a good trip."

The blonde flicked Rory an amused glance and

leaned forward to murmur in Caroline's ear. "You, too, kiddo."

"What was that all about?" Rory wanted to know as Caro hurried away.

"Girl talk. I hear you're staying in Spain another night. What's up?"

"Just some loose ends I need to take care."

With a sardonic smile, Sondra nodded to a woman disappearing around a bend in the corridor. "Is that one of those loose ends?"

"Could be."

His European section chief cocked her head and studied him with assessing eyes. "She's not like us, Rory. Hard and tough and cynical."

"You think?"

"I'm just saying you might have to alter your approach."

"Thanks for the advice. I've got it covered."

Or at least he hoped he did. He hadn't needed Sondra to tell him Caroline required a different approach, much less Harry's blunt warning that he'd better not hurt her again. Rory made it a point to learn from past mistakes.

And God knew he'd screwed up the first time around with Caroline. Literally. He'd taken what she'd offered, climbed on his beat-up Ducati and hit the road without a backward glance.

This time, he intended to give her the hearts and flowers she didn't think she deserved.

As he took Sondra's bag and accompanied her to the wrap-up session, he reviewed his carefully devised plans for the coming evening. Satisfied he'd covered every base, Rory switched mental gears from a romantic candlelit dinner for two to the grim realities of high-profile kidnappings and murdered hostages.

Caroline spent the better part of the afternoon confirming flights and ensuring the conferees had transportation to Barcelona to make their scheduled departures.

Harry Martin was one of the last to leave. He and Caro had been forced to make several increasingly exasperated phone calls to Captain Medina, but they'd finally gotten the exit permits squared away. The small arsenal of high-tech weapons Harry had shipped in was now on its way to the airport.

Shoving his Ray-Bans up to rest atop his wiry buzz cut, the retired cop took her hand in a thorny palm. "We got a lot done this week thanks to you, Caroline."

"I'd say it was a joint effort."

"I'll put the word out about EBS when I get home. Should bring you some business from other security companies."

"Thanks, I appreciate that."

"What's your next gig?"

"My partner got a call from a publisher who wants to set up a European book tour for one of their big authors. Ten days, twelve cities and who knows how many TV and radio interviews. I may take that job."

Actually, there wasn't much "may" about it. Sabrina was just about to open their Rome office and Logan Aerospace work would keep Devon busy indefinitely. European Business Services, Inc., would have to think about hiring additional help soon.

The prospect sent a little thrill through Caro's veins. She and her two friends had launched EBS less than a year ago. Yet they'd already recouped their initial investment and were showing a small but steady profit. A few more contracts like Logan Aerospace and GSI and they could start thinking investment strategies and 401(k)s. No small consideration for three women who had walked away from steady jobs with solid retirement plans.

"I heard Rory changed his return reservations," Harry commented.

"You're the second person who's mentioned that to me," she responded dryly. "Does everyone in the personal security business keep track of everyone else's moves?"

"Only those who want to stay alive."

With that careless comment, he slid his sunglasses down to the bridge of his nose.

"Just remember what I told you at the start of the conference. He's a good man."

"You're the second person who's made *that* point today, too."

"Well, there you go. See you around, Caroline."

* * *

Instead of reassuring her, the personal testimonials from Sondra and Harry made Caro nervous. She didn't know what Rory planned to spring on her at dinner tonight, but she suspected it was more than a Valentine's Day card.

What made her even more nervous was that she had no idea what her response would be to whatever he wanted to discuss. She hadn't had time to sort through the wildly conflicting emotions a night in his arms had spawned.

As she took the elevator to her floor, she was forced to admit last night's experiment had failed. Instead of working through her unresolved feelings for Rory, she now had a whole new set to deal with. Not the least of which was the insidious, irrepressible hope that they would end this night naked and sweaty.

Once in her room, she wavered between dressing up and dressing down for the dinner. The voice message Rory had left on her room phone suggesting she wear something warm enough for a walk on the seawall settled the matter.

February days on the Costa Brava could bring enticing sunshine. Nights got a good bit cooler. Especially when the moonlight lured you down to the beach, the undertow sucked you in and you ended up with seaweed in your hair. Lips pursed, Caroline vowed she wouldn't take another dunking tonight.

She kept on the black crinkle skirt but traded the

tangerine cotton tunic for a long-sleeved, cream-colored silk blouse and a wide black belt. The fringed shawl she'd purchased in Tossa de Mar's open-air market provided both a touch of exotic color and the required warmth. Draping one end over her shoulder, Caroline grabbed her purse and took the elevator to the lobby.

Rory was waiting for her. He still wore his dark slacks, now paired with a black turtleneck and a rust-colored sport coat almost the same shade as the ring around his irises.

She thought he might suggest a drink in the hotel bar, but he obviously had other plans.

"You sure you'll be warm enough in that?" he asked, eyeing her shawl.

"I should be. Unless," she added on an after-thought, "you've made reservations at one of Tossa's outdoor restaurants."

"As a matter of fact, we will be eating outside. I requested patio heaters, though."

"Then I'll be fine."

He took her arm and steered her toward the walkway leading down to the seawall. The air was cool but not damp and biting, with just enough breeze to flutter the ends of the shawl.

They joined the others out for an evening stroll on the flat, wide seawall. Their footsteps echoed on the glazed tiles left over from the days of Roman occupation.

The tide was in, Caroline saw. Waves foamed over the shore and lapped at the boats drawn up on the beach and anchored to rings at the base of the seawall. Protected from the sea by the stone walkway, Tossa's trendy hotels and restaurants spilled light, laughter and music into the night.

"Where are we going?" she asked after they'd passed the last establishments.

"Near the base of the castle."

She peered ahead and saw only a faint flicker of light. "There's a restaurant at the base of the cliff? I don't remember seeing one. Only the ruins of a Roman villa."

"That's where we're headed."

"The villa? You're kidding!"

"Nope. The manager at the resort told me they often cater private parties there. He swears it's the most romantic spot in Tossa."

She felt obliged to issue another protest. "I told you this morning I don't need romantic gestures. They're superfluous, given our situation."

"What situation is that, Caroline?"

"You want me to spell it out? All right, I will. Last night was…last night. I didn't expect you to stay in Tossa another night, and I certainly don't expect you to wine me and dine me. Tomorrow we'll fly back to separate homes in separate states. Let's not complicate matters."

"There's nothing that says this has to be the end

of it," he countered. "You told me this morning you wanted to get me out of your system. What if I don't want to get you out of mine?"

"Are you referring to your ridiculous notion that you need to make up for what happened when we were kids?"

"In part," he admitted. "There's more, though. Why don't we talk about it over dinner."

Caroline squashed her doubts and yielded. When they took the stairs leading down from the seawall and stepped through the remains of an arched entryway, she stopped dead.

A linen-draped table sat in solitary splendor in what she guessed was once a mosaic-tiled courtyard. Hundreds of votive candles drenched the scene in soft light. Beyond the circle of their glow, the one wall of the ancient villa still standing provided a stark, dramatic backdrop against the night sky.

"I don't believe this!"

"Believe it," Rory returned with a smile. "The resort manager says they have to get special permission from the Department of Antiquities to set up here. It's worth the effort, don't you think?"

"And then some!"

She'd never eaten in such a historic setting before. This one, she knew from her guidebook, was the real thing—the seaside vacation home of a wealthy Roman merchant who'd found the climate in Tossa very much to his liking.

A waiter materialized out of the darkness beyond the glow of the votives. "Good evening, Senõr Burke. Your table is waiting."

He led them to the solitary table set with fine china and crystal. When he seated Caroline, she noted the rose beside her plate. A red bow was tied around the stem, with the ends of the ribbon trailing across the snowy tablecloth.

As Rory settled into the seat next to hers, Caro fingered the velvety-soft petals with a funny little pang just under her ribs. Okay, so maybe she wasn't as immune to mushy romantic gestures as she thought.

Another waiter appeared then and switched on the umbrella-shaped heater Rory had requested. It shed both light and a soft warmth that enveloped them in a sphere of their own. The second waiter proceeded to fill their water glasses while the first plucked a bottle of champagne out of a silver ice bucket, wiped it with a napkin and held it out for Rory's inspection and approval.

"Champagne," Caroline murmured when the waiter had filled her crystal flute. "A table overlooking the sea. Our own private waitstaff. All we need now is a string quartet."

"It's not a quartet, but..."

At Rory's signal, another figure stepped out of the shadows. Caro's jaw dropped as he tucked a guitar under his arm and strummed the strings with a flourish.

When the opening chords of "Grenada" soared into the night, she turned to her dinner companion in sheer disbelief.

"Hey," he said with a grin, "if you're gonna do something, you might as well do it right."

She waited until the song had spun to a glorious finish, and they'd applauded the performance to follow up on his comment.

"What, exactly, are you trying to do?"

"Set the stage."

"For?"

"For this."

While the guitarist strummed another song, Rory slid a small package wrapped in turquoise paper and tied with a silver ribbon across the table.

"What is it?" Caro asked suspiciously.

"Your Valentine's Day present. I picked it up at the hotel this morning."

Her stomach did a quick flip-flop when she saw the embossed foil sticker on the package. She thought he'd hit the hotel's flower shop. Instead, he'd made a detour into Cartier.

A dozen objections leaped into her mind. Their relationship was too confused, too uncertain, for expensive gifts. More to the point, one night of hedonistic sex did not require a trip to Cartier. Unless he was trying to salve his conscience, she rationalized uneasily. Or pay for services rendered.

As quickly as the thought formed, she dismissed it. Rory wouldn't be that crass.

Or would he?

There was the problem in a nutshell. She didn't really know this man, and she certainly didn't understand why he'd gone to so much trouble to arrange this moonlit dinner. Despite the testimonials from Harry and Sondra, despite the hours they'd spent in each other's arms, he was still an enigma to her.

"I can't accept this, whatever it is."

"Why don't you open it before you decide?"

Taking her lower lip between her teeth, Caroline untied the bow and slid a nail under the foil sticker. Her uneasiness increased when the wrapping paper fell away to reveal a small, square jewelry box.

Okay. All right. No need to make such a big deal. The box could contain earrings. Gold studs, maybe. Or a pin. A pretty bauble to commemorate their trip to Barcelona.

As if she needed a reminder. One glance at Rory's strong, square jaw brought an instant tingle to the various body parts his stubbly bristle had scraped. With a conscious effort of will, Caroline resisted the urge to finger the whisker burn on the side of her neck.

"Shall I serve the *tapas*, sir?"

Rory dismissed the waiter who appeared at the table with a smile. "Give us a few minutes."

The waiter faded into the night. The guitarist continued to strum a Spanish folk song, and Caroline continued to stare at the jewelry box with a mix of wariness and indecision. Finally, her dinner companion assumed the initiative.

"Here. Let me."

When Rory flipped up the lid, Caroline's breath caught in her throat. Nestled in a bed of black velvet was a perfect, heart-shaped emerald edged on one side by diamonds that sparkled even in the dim light. She watched, speechless, as he removed the ring from its case.

"As soon as I saw this, I knew I had to get it for you."

Smiling, he reached for her left hand. Before she could recover enough to whip it away, he slid the ring onto her finger.

"It's a little loose. We'll have to get it sized."

"I can't accept this!"

"Sure you can."

"It's too expensive."

"Not for my fiancée."

Her startled glance shot from the glowing emerald to his face. "Your what?"

"That's my clumsy way of asking you to marry me, Caroline."

Eight

"You've got to be kidding!"

That wasn't exactly the most sophisticated response to a proposal, but it was the best Caroline could manage at the moment.

Smiling at her slack-jawed surprise, Rory brushed his thumb over the back of her hand. "Trust me, I'm a hundred percent serious."

"You can't be! We…We don't see each other for more than ten years, you hear about me secondhand or thirdhand through the wife of a prospective client, we spend a few days together and… Oh!"

She jerked her hand free of his hold. The surprise leached out of her. Understanding and the beginning of a healthy anger seeped in.

"Of course. I forgot. You always pay your debts."

She'd been closer to the truth a few moments ago than she'd realized! He *was* paying for services rendered. Only she'd provided these services more than a decade ago. Her jaw tight, she yanked off the ring and jammed it back into the box. The lid closed with a snap.

"I thought I made myself clear the day you arrived in Tossa. What's done is done. We can't change the past, and I sure as hell don't expect you to—to…" She waved a hand in the air, searching for the right phrase. "To make restitution at this late date."

"What makes you think this is all about the past?"

"Oh, right." Her lip curled. "After one night together, you've fallen hopelessly in love and decided you can't live without me."

His grin slipped out. "You have to admit it was a pretty spectacular night."

"If this is a joke," she snapped, "I don't find it particularly funny."

Sobering, he shook his head. "It's no joke. I told you, I'm dead serious. I want to marry you, Caroline."

"Why?"

"Why not?" he countered. "The heat's still there, even after more than a decade. We haven't found anyone else in all that time. And…"

He paused, his eyes holding hers in the flickering light of the votives. The waiters hovered just out of sight. The guitar player still strummed his instrument, his soft rhythm a counterpoint to the restless waves washing against the seawall.

But it might have been just the two of them, alone in the night, with only the small jewelry box between them.

"I want you, Caroline. After last night, you have to know how much. And I want a family. A wife. Something besides an empty condo to come home to. Kids if we get lucky again."

She flinched, and Rory muttered a curse.

"I'm sorry. That was a poor choice of words. But hearing you'd lost a baby, my baby, made me take a hard look at what I've done with my life—and the changes I need to make in it."

He gathered her hand in his again and raised it to his lips. The utter sincerity in his eyes blunted Caroline's anger even as the brush of his mouth against her skin sent a ripple down her spine.

"I've been pretty much on my own since I was sixteen. Let me come home to you, sweetheart."

The quiet words took her back to that long-ago summer. She could see him in her mind's eye, eighteen again, flexing his muscles under his stained white T-shirt. So cocky, so self-confident and so very much alone.

"You talk about want, Rory. Need. Someone to come home to. What about love? Doesn't that figure anywhere in the equation?"

"The way I see it, they all add up to the same thing."

She had to give him credit for honesty. If pressed, Caroline would have a tough time defining the fragile, illusive emotion poets wrote about herself.

She also had to give him points for the most romantic proposal *ever!* Here they were, seated at the only table set up amid the ruins of a two-thousand-year-old villa, with the moon overhead and guitar music floating through the night.

Caroline couldn't imagine how he'd had time to arrange all this, but she knew that whatever her answer to his astonishing proposal, this Valentine's Day would remain seared in her memory for the rest of her life.

Like that night beside the river.

And the cold, rainy day she'd buried her still-born child.

With a small jolt, she realized this man had figured in two of the three major turning points in her life.

The third was the year she'd spent at the University of Salzburg with Devon and Sabrina. Her friends taught her to laugh again during that year.

Yet not until last night, in Rory's arms, had a part of her she'd thought long dead come alive again. And now… Just the feel of his hand holding hers, the brush of his lips on her skin, sent heat rippling through her veins.

Was he right? Did need and want and love all add up to the same thing? If so, Caroline was knee-deep in the volatile mix for the first time in longer than she could remember.

"Tell you what," Rory said, breaking into her thoughts. "Why don't you defer giving me an answer until after dinner? Or better yet, until tomorrow. I'll use the rest of the night to convince you to say yes."

As if the music and the stars and the churning sea weren't enough! He had to add a husky promise of things to come, which tightened the muscles low in Caroline's belly.

"Tomorrow works for me," she replied, taking the coward's way out. She suspected she would need at least that long, if not longer, to wrap her mind around this extraordinary proposal.

"Good. And until then…" He opened the box and slid the heart-shaped emerald over her knuckle. "So you can get used to the feel of it."

He sat back and signaled the waiter. While they conferred, Caroline tilted her hand until the ring caught the glow of the candles. She was no expert on jewelry by any means. Her biggest splurge to date was a twisted silver bracelet she'd bargained hard for in Mexico. But this…

She didn't need the Cartier box to suspect the ring was light-years away from anything she could afford. The center stone glowed a rich, dark green. The smaller diamonds along the outer edge of the heart sparkled with a brilliance that suggested they cost as much or more than the emerald.

"More champagne, madame?"

With a nod to the waiter, Caroline gave herself up to the evening Rory had gone to such trouble to arrange.

The magic didn't end with dinner.

After coffee and dessert under the stars, they strolled back to the resort along the wide seawall. The wind had picked up, and over Caro's protests, Rory draped his sport coat over her shoulders.

His warmth wrapped around her like a protective shield. His scent teased her senses. As they approached the lights of the resort, his husky promise of things to come had her almost quivering with anticipation.

The anticipation increased exponentially when they took the elevator to his top-floor suite. Rory made maximum use of the short ride by propping a hand against the elevator's paneled wall and leaning in for a kiss.

It started light—a brush of his mouth against hers. It finished with Caroline's hands hooked in his belt, dragging him closer. When the door pinged open, they were both breathing hard and fast.

Thank God his suite was directly opposite the elevator. Caro could barely wait for him to put his key in the door lock. She didn't know whether it was the ridiculously romantic evening he'd orchestrated or the fact that this was their last night together that drove her to such a fever of impatience. Whatever the reason, she couldn't wait for him to flick on the lights.

A warm glow filled the suite. Caroline swept the spacious rooms with a quick glance, taking in once again the rich furnishings, the watercolors decorating the walls, the desk now covered by his open briefcase and a scattering of papers. She also noted the suitcase sitting on the bench at the foot of the bed, waiting to be packed. Spurred by the sight, she went into Rory's arms.

"I have the rest of the night all scripted," he warned between greedy kisses. "Soft music. Cognac. Sipped slowly while enjoying the view of the moon over the bay."

"Does the script end with us getting naked?"

"Of course."

"Forget the music and cognac," she muttered, dragging up the hem of his turtleneck. "I want you without clothes. Now."

As soon as she had his shirt off, her hands went to his belt again. She tugged him toward the bedroom, fumbling with the belt buckle as they went.

He returned the favor by peeling off her shawl and unhooking buttons at the waistband of her long crinkle skirt. By the time she had him backed against the edge of the bed, they'd left their clothing in a haphazard trail from one room to the other.

The embarrassing recollection of how quickly she'd climaxed last night made Caroline determined this session would last considerably longer. She would set the pace, she decided, as she stretched up on tiptoe to lock her mouth with his. She would take him to the edge over and over again and give him at least a partial return on the mindless pleasure he'd given her.

Naked, her body eager and straining against his, she took him down to the bed with her. His weight pinned her, but she wiggled free. Hooking a leg over his, she rolled upright and straddled his hips.

"How about I script the rest of this scene?"

Instant delight glinted in the golden depths of his eyes. "Be my guest."

She could feel him rock hard against her inner thigh. Raising up a few inches, Caroline positioned him between the hot folds of her flesh. Slowly, so slowly, she slid her hips back. Forward. Back again.

The erotic friction closed her throat and kicked her heart into a wild rhythm faster than any flamenco. Her body secreted a warm, wet lubricant in response to the movement. His did the same. Their fluids joined as she increased both the tempo and the pressure.

Rory didn't remain passive for long. His hands slicked over her hips and roamed the curve of her waist before moving to her breasts. He kneaded the soft flesh, then rolled the nipples between his thumbs and forefingers until they'd stiffened to hard peaks.

"I want to taste you, Caroline."

Panting now, she leaned forward and dug her hands into the mattress on either side of his head. The sparkling diamonds edging the emerald distracted her for a second or two. Just until Rory took one aching nipple in his mouth. Alternately sucking and rasping with his teeth and tongue, he generated a series of intense sensations that jolted throughout Caroline's body.

Soon even those incredible sensations weren't enough. She wanted him inside her. Every steely inch. She shifted her hips to one side, but Rory caught her hand as she reached down to position the tip.

"Let me get some protection."

"It's okay," she muttered, too hot to wait. "I'm taking birth control."

"But last night…"

"Double indemnity."

She already had the tip partially in. A slight hitch of her hips and it slid deeper. With a sound that was halfway between a sigh and a groan, she sank lower.

Hazy sunlight crept through the shutters when Caroline drifted awake the next morning.

Gradually she registered the fact that she lay sprawled in hedonistic abandon across Rory's chest. Her left leg was thrown over his. Her arm was hooked over his waist. With a little smacking sound from her dry lips, she snuggled closer.

A large hand stroked her hair, slowly and lazily. Minutes passed in boneless contentment, then Rory's deep voice pulled Caroline from a light doze.

"Well? What's the verdict?"

"The verdict?" She raised her head and gave him a sleepy smile. "Best sex I ever had. Except maybe for the other night in Barcelona."

Laughter rumbled up from his chest. "Happy to be of service, ma'am."

Bending an elbow atop her chest, she propped her chin on her hand. God, he looked good in the morning! Especially with that prickly blond stubble shading his chin and amusement crinkling the skin at the corners of his eyes.

"That wasn't the verdict I was looking for, though."

"Mmm?"

"Did I convince you to say yes?"

Lost in contemplation of his whiskery chin and smiling eyes, it took a moment for the question to register. When it did, she eased into a sitting position and hitched the sheet under her arms.

Rory had gone all out with his over-the-top, romantic proposal. The Roman villa, the guitar, the flickering votives. Caroline had been too surprised, too overwhelmed to think straight last night. In the hazy light of dawn, her more cautious self prevailed.

"I jumped in feetfirst with you once and paid the price," she said, searching for the right words. "I need to… We *both* need to proceed more deliberately this time. Explore our feelings. See if they take us anywhere besides bed."

He waggled his brows in an exaggerated leer. "Let's hope they don't take us anywhere else."

"I'm serious, Rory. I want to slow this train down."

"Okay, I hear you." Frowning, he scraped a palm across his bristles. "Exploration could be a little difficult, though, since you live in Virginia and I operate out of California."

"Difficult but not impossible. Unless you think what we might have together isn't worth the effort."

"Oh, you're worth it. You're most definitely worth it. But I have to warn you that patience isn't my strongest suit. When I decide I want something, I go after it."

"I noticed," she drawled. "So we're agreed? We slow things down?"

"We might have to define 'slow' more precisely," he warned with a quick glance at the digital clock beside the bed. "How about we discuss it during the ride to the airport?"

Nodding, Caroline slid the heart-shaped emerald off her finger and held it out to him. Rory refused to take it.

"It's yours, sweetheart. I want you to keep it as a reminder of your night out in Tossa."

Like she could ever forget it?

After she retreated to her own room to shower and pack, Caroline took a moment to stand at the window before going downstairs. A thin fog had rolled in off the sea, almost obscuring the castle at the far end of the seawall. Below the castle, the one remaining wall of the Roman villa stood like a sentinel in the mist.

Until last night, she would have said her favorite spot in Europe was and always would be Salzburg. This small resort on Spain's Costa Brava now vied with the Austrian city for first place in her heart.

Sighing, she grabbed the handle on her roller suitcase and slung the strap of her briefcase over her shoulder. A few moments later she stepped out of the elevator directly across from the resort's business offices. Her last task was to go over the final charge sheet with the conference planner.

The planner was as efficient as she was observant. While Caroline reviewed the carefully tallied charges, the woman eyed her left hand.

"Your ring is very beautiful," she commented in the musical dialect of the Catalan region.

"Thank you."

"Did you buy it here, in Tossa?"

"No, I, or rather, Mr. Burke, purchased it in Barcelona. It was, uh, a Valentine's Day gift."

"Mr. Burke? The gentleman who arranged the special dinner last night?"

"Yes."

To Caroline's utter mortification, a wave of heat rushed into her cheeks. The blush won a smile from the woman on the other side of the desk.

"Ah. He is very romantic. My husband gave me

only roses and chocolates." Her dark eyes twinkled. "You must come back to Tossa for your honeymoon, yes?"

Mumbling a noncommittal response, Caro signed the charge sheet. She could still feel the embarrassed heat in her cheeks when she took the elevator to the lobby.

Rory was waiting for her at the front desk. He'd dressed casually for the long flight back to LA in jeans, an open-necked shirt and the rust-colored sport coat he'd worn last night.

"I called Delta and had them upgrade your ticket," he informed her as the valet had stowed their suitcases in the trunk of his rented BMW.

"Why did you do that?"

"It's a long flight. You might as well go first-class. I fly all my key people first-class," he added before she could object.

That was true. Caro should know. She'd worked their reservations herself. Still, she felt compelled to point out she didn't qualify as a "key" GSI person.

Unperturbed, Rory tipped the valet. "That's one of those minor details we need to work out. I may have agreed to a long-distance courtship, but I haven't agreed to the terms. Yet."

"Good thing we've got this drive to the airport," Caroline retorted. "Looks like we may have to enter into some heavy negotiations."

* * *

The negotiations ate up a good forty minutes of the trip into Barcelona, primarily because they veered off on multiple tangents.

Topics they hadn't had a chance to discuss came up. Like music and favorite movies and food preferences. Caro admitted to being an opera buff, watching *Phantom of the Opera* every time it popped up on TV and liking her steak rare. Rory preferred bluesy jazz and—of course—Tom Clancy's books and movies.

He'd just confessed a passion for crunchy fried fish when his cell phone rang. Keeping one hand on the wheel, he dug the instrument out of his shirt pocket and flipped up the lid.

"Burke."

Even Caro could hear the high, wailing cry that came through the earpiece.

"You must help us! My husband has been kidnapped!"

Nine

While Caroline sat frozen in the BMW's passenger seat, Rory gripped the steering wheel with one hand and jammed his cell phone against his ear with the other.

"Who is this?"

"Elena!" the woman wailed. "Elena Casteel."

"How do you know your husband's been kidnapped?"

Rory kept his tone deliberate and steady in direct contrast to Señora Casteel's shrill panic.

"Juan called! He told me they took him and his driver! Then someone snatched the phone away. He said I'll find Juan's head on the front steps if I don't pay them twenty million euros!"

"When did you get the call?"

"A half hour ago. Perhaps less. I don't know." Her voice spiraled into a terrified sob. "They said I must not notify the police or alert the media! They'll kill Juan if I do!"

Rory had enough experience with executive kidnappings to know whoever had snatched Casteel wouldn't hesitate to follow through on that threat. He'd also bet they were monitoring the phones and listening to his wife's every word.

"I found your business card on my husband's desk," she cried. "He told me you're good, Señor Burke. He said you know a great deal about this awful business. Please, please! You must help me!"

Rory didn't remind the distraught woman her husband had purchased kidnapping and ransom insurance. Or that the highly specialized insurance company would most likely send in a team of experts to handle the negotiations. No need to alert anyone who might be listening in that Casteel had prepared for this situation. The knowledge would only prolong the negotiations.

Besides, Rory knew from past experience the first few hours in any kidnapping were the most crucial. Confused and frightened, relatives often made decisions that led to disastrous consequences. Until the insurance team arrived, Elena Casteel would need someone on the scene who understood the life-and-death game that kidnappers played.

"Of course I'll help you."

He raked a quick glance at the road ahead. They'd already passed the expressway leading into the city center, but he spotted an exit just ahead and cut the steering wheel. Tires screeched, and a wide-eyed Caroline snatched at the armrest to keep from slamming against the passenger door.

"You caught me on my way into Barcelona," he told Elena. "I'm about twenty minutes away. Your husband's right," he added in an attempt to steady her for the ordeal he knew would follow. "I have a great deal of experience in this terrible business. I'll help you get through it."

"And you'll bring Juan home safe?"

He refused to make promises he couldn't keep and dodged the question.

"You'd better leave the phone line open. If the kidnappers call again before I get there, write down the instructions they give you. Every word. Understand?"

"Yes."

"Is there anyone else at the house who could help you?"

"Only the servants and I'm afraid to tell them about Juan. They might call someone, say something."

"What about a friend? A relative?"

"No, no!" Her despair poured through the phone. "There is no one!"

"Okay, Elena. It's okay. I promise you won't go through this alone."

He saw Caroline pointing urgently at an overhead sign and whipped the wheel again.

"Hang on. I'm just turning onto Avenue Meridiana. I'll be there shortly."

She sobbed her thanks and cut the connection. Rory snapped his cell phone shut, his mind already in high gear.

From the time he'd spent with Juan Casteel, he knew the shipping magnate was extremely security conscious. He kept his picture and that of his wife out of the newspapers. He varied his schedule and route to work every day. He'd sent his chauffeur for special training and had installed high-tech systems to protect both his home and his office. That person or persons unknown had penetrated his security measures suggested that this wasn't a quick snatch by street thugs taking a target of opportunity. It was a well-planned abduction.

The twenty-million-euro ransom also suggested the kidnapping wasn't political. Political kidnappings usually involved a demand for a release of prisoners. *Usually* being the operative word, as a growing number of terrorist groups worldwide were turning to high-dollar kidnappings to finance their operations.

He had to talk to Elena and hear the exact details of the ransom demand before he could get a fix on the situation. And before he did *that,* he needed to hustle Caroline out of the picture.

One glance at her shocked face told him she'd heard enough of his side of the conversation to know exactly what was going down.

"I'll drop you off at a hotel," he told her tersely. "Take a cab to the airport. When you get there, cancel my flight and notify the rental agency that I'm keeping the car indefinitely."

Her brow creased. Rory guessed what was coming before she made a tentative suggestion.

"I don't want to get in the way, but maybe I can help. It sounds like Elena's alone. If nothing else, I could hold her hand while you deal with the kidnappers."

"You don't want to get in the middle of this, Caroline. The tension, the gut-wrenching fear... They wring even trained professionals inside out. And if it goes bad," he added, his jaw tight, "the nightmares will haunt you."

She nodded, acknowledging the grim possibilities, but didn't shrink from them.

"I've had a taste of tension and fear. Not to this extent, it's true, but enough to know I won't fall apart on you."

The quiet assertion sliced into his racing thoughts. Brought up short, he shot her a hard look.

"Let me help, Rory."

His fist tight on the wheel, he weighed the options. He could use a second set of eyes and ears. He might also need a runner to relay messages in a safe zone, away from the house.

"All right. You're in. On one condition. If the situation looks like it might go south, you do what I say, when I say. No questions, no arguments."

"Agreed."

Fifteen minutes later Rory identified the palatial late-nineteenth-century town house where he and Caroline had dined a few nights ago.

He cruised the block of similar residences, noting how they crowded side by side, with only a narrow gate leading to rear carriage houses that now served as garages. Noting, too, vehicles parked on either side of the tree-lined boulevard.

Word of the kidnapping hadn't leaked. There were no police cruisers, no TV crews in sight. Nor any delivery vans or cars with darkened windows. No suspicious vehicles of any sort.

Still, the skin at the back of Rory's neck tingled as he pulled into a space halfway down the block. The kidnappers were watching. They had to be watching. Or they had an inside man to keep tabs on the wife. The possibility coiled Rory's gut into a tight knot.

"You sure you want to do this?" he asked Caroline when they exited the BMW. "It's not too late to jump in a cab and catch your flight back to the States."

"I'm sure."

He skimmed another glance down the street. A young au pair strolled along the opposite sidewalk, leading a toddler by the hand. Two older women walked arm in arm on this side of the street. Bundled in coats and scarves and hats despite the mild February weather, they had their heads together and chatted nonstop. Farther down the block a gardener trimmed the bushes in front of a majestic home.

So calm. So normal. So potentially treacherous.

"Here's the deal," he told Caroline as they approached the Casteels' residence. "The kidnappers may have someone on the inside. Someone who fed them information on Juan's personal habits and travel plans. We'll have to run background checks on the entire staff. Until they're vetted, be careful what you say."

She paled a little but nodded. "I will."

"We also have to assume that the house may be bugged. Or the kidnappers may have set up electronic listening posts. Don't use the house phone or your cell phone to discuss anything related to the kidnapping until we get someone in to conduct a sweep. Got that?"

"Got it."

Hoping to hell he wasn't putting her in danger, Rory rang the bell.

The security cameras swept them, and Elena Casteel herself answered the door. Their sophisticated hostess of a few nights ago had disintegrated into a shaking, white-faced wreck. She didn't question Caroline's presence as she ushered them into the foyer.

"I sent the servants home," she said, clutching a handkerchief in one trembling fist. "The cook, the maid, the gardener... I told them I was sick. That was... That was right, wasn't it?"

"That's fine, but we'll want to talk to them later. And we'll need their names and addresses to run through our databases."

"You don't think... You can't think..." Ashen-faced, she wadded the handkerchief into a tight ball. "Our cook's been with us for ten years. Paolo, the gardener, for three or four. The maid...Maria... She's Paolo's daughter."

"We just need to cover all bases," Rory said gently. "How about we sit down? I want you to tell me what was said in the phone call you received. Word for word."

"Yes. Of course."

Elena led the way into a sitting room decorated with Tiffany lamps and art-nouveau-style furnishings. Her lace-trimmed handkerchief fluttered as she made a pitiful attempt to play the hostess.

"Would you care for a cup of tea? I was just about to make a pot. To steady my nerves," she added with what she no doubt hoped was a smile.

The valiant, if completely unsuccessful, attempt tugged at Caroline's heart. "Why don't I take care of that?" she suggested.

The older woman's eyes flooded with grateful tears. "Thank you. The kitchen is just beyond the dining room. There's tea in the caddy. And coffee. Espresso, if you prefer it."

The Casteels' kitchen blended belle-epoch grandeur and modern convenience with seamless artistry. As in the other rooms in the house, the vaulted ceiling was at least fourteen feet high and crowned with ornately carved medallion. The wrought-iron light fixtures featured Tiffany-style shades and complemented the wrought-iron table and chairs set in a window nook that overlooked the garden.

Caroline dropped her purse on an island counter containing a carousel of spice bottles and a gleaming, stainless-steel espresso maker. The appliance drew a look of intense longing, but she reminded herself that Elena had expressed a desire for tea.

A quick check of the cupboards produced the tea caddy, a heating coil to boil water and a tray for the china cups and saucers she extracted from a glass-fronted hutch. She was slicing a lemon for the tea when the sudden jangle of a cell phone nearly made her jump out of her skin.

For a startled moment she thought it was the kidnappers trying to contact Elena. Only on the second ring did she realize the sound emanated from her purse.

With a muttered curse, she dropped the knife and dug out her cell phone. Rory's grim warning replayed in her mind as she checked the number on the display screen.

Oh, Lord! Sabrina!

Caroline had completely forgotten her promise to check in with her partners before she boarded her plane to the States.

The phone gave another insistent buzz. Scrambling to figure out what she could and couldn't say, Caro flipped up the lid.

"Hi, Sabrina."

"Hey, girl! Inquiring minds want to know. How did it go last night?"

Last night? Her mind went blank for a moment before she remembered the Roman villa and the guitarist. This morning's events had shoved the entire evening right out of her head.

"Look, this isn't a good time to discuss last night. I'll give you an update when…"

"Oh, no! You're not getting off the hook that easily. Come on, Caro. Spill it. What did you decide to do vis-à-vis the ghost from your past?"

"I really can't talk about that right now."

"Why? Is he there with you?"

"No. Well, yes. Listen, Sabrina, I'm not flying home today."

"Huh?"

"Something's come up. I'll tell you about it when I can. Right now I just need you to do me a favor and cancel my reservations. Rory's, too. *Please.*"

The touch of desperation in her voice got through to her partner.

"I'll take care of it," Sabrina said slowly, "but…"

"I have to go. I'll call you when I can."

Caro snapped down the lid. Planting her palms on the counter, she pulled in several shaky breaths. Less than a half hour into this frightening situation and her nerves were already strung wire-tight. And it wasn't her husband being held hostage!

Wondering how in the world Elena would hold up through this awful ordeal, she went back to slicing lemons.

A half hour later Rory had wrung every detail he could from Elena. Leaving her with Caroline, he slipped out the back way and over a garden wall. Once he was out of range of any listening devices, he made three calls.

His first was to a contact at Interpol. Although the kidnappers had warned Elena not to notify the police, Rory knew they would be alerted by the large cash withdrawals required for the ransom. Albért Boudoin, chief of the Kidnapping and Ransom Unit at Interpol, was just the man to coordinate with the Spanish authorities and keep them out of sight.

His second call was to Lloyd's of London, who'd insured Juan Casteel. His third was to Harry Martin.

When he returned a short time later, he sat with Elena and Caroline in the sun-drenched kitchen. His rock-solid calm helped both women through the tense hours that followed.

Around three that afternoon, Rory's cell phone buzzed. He checked the number on caller ID and went out the back door again. He returned a short time later with two men and one woman.

After conducting an electronic sweep of the house and phone lines, the Lloyd's of London team of specialists disabled a jury-rigged wiretap. They then sat down with Rory and Elena for another exhaustive review of the details known so far.

"We agree with Mr. Burke," the team leader concluded. "This doesn't look like an express kidnapping. Your husband wasn't snatched off the street by chance, Mrs. Casteel. The job was well planned and executed."

The second call from the kidnappers substantiated the collective opinion.

It came just past ten that evening. Once again the caller's voice was electronically disguised to strip it of any identifying characteristics. He—or she—flatly refused to negotiate the twenty-million ransom and issued precise instructions as to the denomination, sequencing and delivery of the euro banknotes.

As proof of life, the caller put Juan on the phone for all of ten or fifteen seconds. Just long enough to reassure his wife and rip out her heart at the same time.

"I love you, *querida*. Whatever happens, always remember that I love you."

Elena collapsed after the call. Luckily, the Lloyd's

of London unit included a trained counselor. He consoled the sobbing wife while Rory and the other team members made arrangements for the ransom and discussed options for its delivery.

Caroline made a conscientious effort to stay out of their way but found plenty to do. As the night progressed, the team required endless pots of coffee. And sandwiches. Heaping platters of sandwiches. Thank God the Casteels' cook had stocked the pantry with a loaf of crusty Spanish bread and the fridge with an assortment of meats and cheese.

By three in the morning, Caroline was intimately familiar with every nook and cranny in the Casteels' kitchen. By four, she was feeling the effects of the long day and two—correction, make that three— exhausting nights. Her shoulders slumping, she perched on one of the stools at the kitchen island and sipped a cup of espresso.

"You look beat."

Rory's comment brought her around on the stool. He'd shed his sport coat hours ago and rolled up the sleeves of his once-pristine shirt. The wrinkles in the pale blue cotton matched the tired lines in his face.

"You don't look much better," Caroline observed.

"Yeah, I know. Elena offered us the use of a guest room. Why don't you go upstairs and get some rest?"

"Are you going up?"

"In a while. Maybe."

"How about Elena?"

"She says she couldn't sleep and doesn't want to try." He hooked his chin toward Caro's coffee cup. "Any more where that came from?"

"There is. Sit for a minute, and I'll brew you up some. You want it with or without milk?"

"Without."

When the espresso machine hissed out a stream of dark, scalding liquid, Caro slid the cup along the counter. Rory reached for it gratefully and cradled it in his hands.

The faint webbing of scars drew her gaze. She understood now why he would bust out a window with his bare hands. The Casteels weren't even his clients, yet he hadn't hesitated to respond to Elena's frantic call for help.

He'd been so good with her. So calm and steady and comforting. As Sondra Jennings had said, he was the kind of man any woman would want to have watching her back.

The kind of man who, if he'd known about the baby all those years ago, would have stood square-shouldered beside Caro when she faced her parents. Her pastor. Her high school counselor. Her sniggering friends.

And there, in the Casteels' dim kitchen, with Rory hunkered on a stool across from her, Caroline felt her last lingering regrets about the past slip quietly away.

* * *

At ten in the morning, Elena, Rory and one member of the K & R team drove to the bank. The bank manager had already been alerted by Lloyd's of London. He had the requested denominations of euros stacked and waiting.

At three that afternoon, Rory prepared to deliver the ransom.

Caroline had expected the negotiations to take much longer. But in the past thirty hours she'd learned her Hollywood-style perceptions of how these matters went down had little basis in reality. The single driving purpose of the Kidnapping and Ransom Unit was to get their client back alive, as quickly as possible.

For that reason, Interpol and the police had remained on the periphery, the negotiations didn't drag on needlessly and no one, least of all the K & R team, proposed any shoot-'em-up attempts to rescue the hostage.

They weren't going to just hand over the cash, of course. Rory's Interpol contact had arranged for the banknotes to be sprayed with a coating that would collect invisible but indelible fingerprints. Additionally, the technician on the K & R team had installed microscopic tracking devices in the duffel bag on wheels, which contained the ransom.

He also inserted a microscopic video camera into one stem of Rory's aviator sunglasses. The device relayed startlingly clear pictures via satellite. So clear that Caroline saw her face displayed in digital high-def on three separate computer screens when Rory drew her aside to tell her not to worry.

"Yeah, like that's going to happen! I still don't see why you have to deliver the ransom," she muttered with a glance at the others. "These people are pros."

She didn't need Rory's wry look to know how foolish that sounded. This was his business, his profession. He'd taken charge from the first hour and had been the unspoken leader of the team since it assembled.

"Do you… Do you really think they'll let Juan and his driver go?"

"It's a business, Caroline. These bastards are professionals. They know the insurance companies will stop paying if they don't deliver the hostages as promised. That's why less than two percent of all kidnappings brokered by K & R units end in death."

"So you said."

Several times in fact. Somehow a ninety-eight percent success rate didn't reassure Caro as much now as it had before the first few times Rory had stated that calm fact. Especially after watching him strap on a shoulder harness and an ankle holster.

Her gaze went to Elena, sitting white-faced and numb across the room. Caro knew the worry and fear gnawing at her insides couldn't come anywhere close to the distraught wife's, but they were enough for her to reach up and frame Rory's face with both hands.

The beginnings of a stubbly beard tickled her palms. The emerald he'd slipped on her finger winked in the afternoon light. Caroline registered neither as she pleaded with him, her voice low and urgent.

"Promise me you'll be careful."

"That goes without saying."

"And when you finish with the kidnappers, we'll resume our own negotiations."

A smile crinkled the skin at the corners of his eyes. Wolf's eyes, she thought, her throat tight. About to search out and stalk down their prey.

"That's right. We still have to work out the details of our long-distance courtship."

"Maybe not so long-distance," she murmured, going up on her toes.

"How's that?"

"We'll talk about it when this is over."

Caroline kissed him, hard, and issued a fierce command.

"Come back to me, Rory. This time, you have to come back."

Ten

Caroline didn't draw a full breath for the next three hours. Fear lodged like a jagged rock in her throat as she watched the startlingly clear images sent back by the camera in Rory's sunglasses.

Following the kidnappers' instructions, he criss-crossed Barcelona. They gave him only minutes to hail a cab and race across town or seconds to jump a subway jammed with rush-hour commuters. Two of the K & R team members had tagged him as far as the subway. They lost him when he joined more than ninety thousand rabid football fans pouring into Barcelona's Camp Nou Stadium.

When he finally made the drop and walked away,

Caroline wanted to weep with relief and whoop with joy. Elena's paper-white face kept her from doing either. Still, she couldn't refrain from wrapping Rory in a ferocious hug when he returned to the Casteels' town house.

After that, there was nothing to do but hover over the computers while the K & R team tracked the ransom's erratic progress across northern Spain. As one agonizing hour followed another, a grim silence gripped the entire team. Caroline made pot after pot of coffee. The little that was left of Elena's nerves shredded, but she refused to take a sedative or lie down.

Then, just before midnight, the phone rang with the call they'd all been waiting for. A truck driver had found Juan Casteel and his chauffeur stumbling along a deserted country road. Their eyes, mouths and hands were duct-taped, and they'd each sustained vicious bruises but were otherwise unhurt.

Rory and three members of the team shot out of the house to work the recovery. Caroline and the fourth team member stayed with the sobbing Elena.

By eight o'clock the following morning, Rory's role in life-and-death drama was over. Except, he informed Caroline wryly, for the paperwork.

The Lloyd's of London team would track and, hopefully, recover the ransom. Interpol would take down the kidnappers when and if the bastards showed their hand. Trained counselors would work with Juan, his driver and Elena to help them through any post-traumatic stress. In response to Rory's call the previous day, Harry Martin flew in two skilled operatives to beef up the Casteels' security and guard against future kidnapping attempts.

"All we have to do now is provide formal statements," Rory told Caroline with tired satisfaction.

"I don't see how I can add anything to the team's collective input."

"You were here. You saw and heard everything. You might have picked up details the rest of us missed."

"Not likely. And the way I feel now, your friend from Interpol isn't going to get much out of me."

"I told Albért we were wiped out. He said he'll contact us tomorrow. Think you can find us a hotel room to crash in?"

"Consider it done."

She called the same hotel they'd stayed in before. To her intense relief, the Hotel Grand Royale had a vacant suite and could accommodate an early-morning check-in.

When a still-weepy but joyous Elena heard they were going to a hotel, she urged them to stay at the town house. Rory declined with a smile.

"You and Juan need this time together."

"But we'll see you again before you leave Barcelona?"

"Most definitely."

When Caroline walked out of the Casteels' residence beside Rory, a sudden feeling of disorientation hit her. Blinking, she surveyed the scene.

Sunlight slanted through the chestnut trees lining the wide boulevard. Birds twittered in the branches. Nannies pushed baby carriages and chattered among themselves.

It was all so normal. So sane. As if the terror and human drama of the past forty-eight hours had never occurred.

She sank into the passenger seat of the BMW and let her head drop back against the padded headrest. She'd gone for most of those forty-eight hours fueled by fear, espresso and a few quick catnaps. Now that Juan was safe and the euphoric elation over his return had ratcheted down, exhaustion was setting in with a vengeance.

She rolled her head to the left. Rory looked about as bad as she felt. If he'd slept at all in the past two days, she didn't know when.

"Thank heavens the hotel can check us in this early." She sighed. "I want a bath, a full breakfast delivered by room service and at least twelve solid hours in bed."

"Twelve, huh?"

"Some of those twelve I need to sleep," she warned. "So do you!"

"Let's see how it goes."

She might have challenged that comment if she wasn't already sinking fast.

Rory nudged her awake at the front entrance to the hotel. With a tight grip on her arm, he sleepwalked her through the revolving doors. She blinked owlishly at the flower shop in the lobby and thought she recognized the paneled entrance to Cartier. The brief stop at the front desk was a total blur, however. So was the elevator ride to their floor.

"Come on, sweetheart. We're almost there."

Rory steered her down a vaguely familiar hallway carpeted in green and gold. A porter followed with the luggage and briefcases they'd packed what now seemed like two lifetimes ago for their flights back to the States.

Caroline had realigned her priorities even before she entered the luxurious suite. "Forget what I said about a bath and room service."

Ignoring the view of the cathedral that had so enchanted her their first night in Barcelona, she aimed straight for the bedroom. She stayed on her feet only long enough to fish her cell phone out of her purse and leave a voice mail for her partner Sabrina.

"I'm at the Hotel Grand Royale in Barcelona," she mumbled. "Don't call me. I'll call you. Tomorrow. After I talk to Interpol."

Maybe she shouldn't have tacked on that last bit, she thought as she flipped the cell phone shut. Oh, well. Too late now, and she was too tired to put together a coherent sentence in any case.

She kicked off her shoes, shed her jacket and dropped facedown into the cotton-covered duvet.

When she swam back to semiconsciousness, the drawn drapes let in only a faint, hazy light. Rory lay beside her, sprawled on his back, his breathing deep and steady.

He'd stripped down to his shorts, Caroline noted sleepily. Stripped her down, too. At least she assumed he'd done the deed. She couldn't remember and didn't particularly care. Hooking an arm over his waist, she snuggled against him and dropped into oblivion again.

When she woke the second time, the room was dark and the bed beside her empty. Only a faint light showed under the door to the sitting room. Rolling over, she squinted at the bedside clock. When she saw the time, a smile tugged at her lips. Almost twelve hours exactly.

After stretching until her joints popped, Caroline rolled out of bed. She spotted her clothes draped over a chair. Her suitcase sat on the bench at the end of the bed, with her purse and briefcase beside it.

She should call her partners. She knew her cryptic messages over the past few days must have them worried. The obnoxious rumble her stomach emitted put phone calls in a distant second place to food! Any kind of food!

Fishing out her toiletries, Caroline hit the bathroom. She emerged a short time later wrapped in one of the hotel's plush robes and marched to the door to the sitting room. With a dramatic gesture, she flung it open.

"Feed me."

Rory looked up from the work he'd spread over the desk. "With pleasure. I thought I would starve waiting for you to wake up."

He'd pulled on a pair of khakis and a long-sleeved shirt with the cuffs rolled up and the tails hanging out. His cheeks still sported a bristly stubble, but Caroline saw—with relief—that his eyes were no longer rimmed red by fatigue.

"Do you want to go out or order from room service?"

Caro's glance went to the terrace doors. They framed the view that had so enchanted her the first night. The brilliantly illuminated spires of Gaudí's Sagrada Familia thrusting into the night sky.

She ached to show Rory more of the Barcelona she loved. The city's many restaurants and *tapas* bars would just be coming to life, she knew, especially along the series of teeming, vibrant, pedestrians-only streets known collectively as La Rambla.

But going out would involve getting dressed, slapping on makeup, waiting an indeterminate period at a crowded restaurant. She was too ravenous for any of the above.

"Let's do room service. If we're still here tomorrow night, I'll take you to my favorite restaurant in the Gothic Quarter."

"Sounds good to me."

From under the papers on the desk he extracted a leather-bound binder embossed with the hotel's insignia.

"Why don't you order while I shower and shave. I would have cleaned up earlier, but you were snuffling and mumbling into the pillow and I didn't want to wake you."

"Mumbling? What about?"

"Most of it was unintelligible. I did catch a phrase or two, though. One was my name. I'm pretty sure the other was 'way hot.'"

"You're making that up."

"Maybe." Grinning, he speared a hand into her wet hair. "And maybe not."

He dropped a kiss on her mouth, scraping her chin with his bristles, and left with instructions to order him a steak, medium rare, with all the trimmings.

Caroline took the menu to a chair beside the unlit fireplace. Her legs curled under her, she pored through the extensive list of offerings. It ran to eighteen pages, with the first five devoted to the hotel's incredible selection of appetizers.

She lined up her choices after a lengthy internal

debate. Carrying the menu back to the desk, she shuffled some of Rory's papers aside and reached for the desk phone. A direct line connected her with room service.

She ordered a rib eye with all the trimmings for Rory, grilled lamb kebabs with rice pilaf for her. A bottle of Spanish red wine to go with them. And *tapas*. Lots of *tapas*. Fifteen scrumptious, bite-size delicacies to celebrate the conclusion of a remarkable day.

"Send the wine and *tapas* up right away," she requested. "We'll enjoy them while we wait for dinner."

"Yes, madame."

Her stomach rumbling in joyous anticipation, Caroline replaced the phone in its cradle and closed the menu. When she realigned Rory's papers, one near the bottom of the pile snagged her attention. She blinked, startled by the header printed in bold letters.

Operation Caroline Walters.

"What the heck…?"

Frowning, she slid the typewritten sheet free of the pile. Utter disbelief swept through her as she skimmed the paragraph headings, also bolded.

Phase One—Scope out the target.
Phase Two—Arrange initial contact.
Phase Three—Initiate contact.
Phase Four…

She hadn't heard the shower cut off, but she did hear the bedroom door open. She spun around, the typewritten sheet clutched in her fist, as Rory strolled in. Like her, he was wrapped in one of the hotel's plush robes. *Unlike* her, he was loose and relaxed.

"Did you put the order in?" he asked, then caught her expression. "What's the matter?"

When she didn't answer, couldn't answer, he strode over to her.

"Caroline, what's happened? Did Albért call? Did they take down the kidnappers?"

"No," she got out through frozen lips. "Your friend at Interpol did not call. And yes, I put the order in. In the process, I found this."

Her arm rigid, she held out the sheet of paper. Rory glanced at it and grimaced.

"Oh, hell! That isn't what it looks like."

"Really?"

Drawing on a lifetime of painful, hard-won experience, Caroline clamped an iron band on her roiling emotions. "You'd better enlighten me. What *is* it?"

"What we used to call an operations plan in the military."

She flipped the paper around and skimmed over the contents again. Phrases leaped out at her. Some typed, some scratched out and rewritten in hand. When she lifted her gaze again, her heart felt like a solid block of ice inside her chest.

"So it *was* all scripted. Just like you said. Every

word. Every touch. That…that elaborate Valentine's Day seduction."

He could hardly deny it, given the evidence in stark black and white.

"I only planned the initial phases. Tracking you down. Steering the conference contract to EBS. Flying over to Spain to…"

"To make things right with me," Caro finished in a harsh, dry whisper.

"I told you that was my intention. I never hid it from you."

"No, you didn't."

"What wasn't scripted, what I didn't intend, was the way you threw me completely off stride. I haven't stuck to the plan since that night on the beach, when the undertow almost sucked you in. Instead, it sucked me in."

His eyes held hers, steady and unrelenting.

"I'm in over my head now, Caroline. Way over my head. I…"

The rap of knuckles against the door to the suite cut him off.

"The *tapas,*" she forced out through a throat that felt etched with glass. "I asked room service to bring them up first."

Rory muttered a curse and strode toward the entryway. It wasn't room service on the other side of the door, however, but a tall, leggy blonde backed by three companions.

"Are you Burke?" she demanded.

"Yes."

"Where's Caroline?"

"She's…"

"I'm right here!"

Reeling from her second shock of the evening, Caro gaped as her two business partners rushed into the suite.

"Sabrina! Devon! What are you two doing here?"

"What do you *think* we're doing here!" Sabrina retorted, enveloping her in a fierce hug.

The tallest of the three partners, she had a tumble of pale blond curls, mile-long legs and an upbeat personality that recognized few obstacles—not the least of which was a domineering father who'd tried repeatedly and unsuccessfully to mold her into a female version of himself.

"You scared the bejesus out of me with your 'I can't talk now' and 'don't call me.' That bit about having to talk to Interpol didn't help, either. You have some serious explaining to do, girlfriend."

Devon appeared no less worried. Her brown eyes were filled with concern under a fringe of auburn bangs. "'Rina called me in London. Cal had his corporate jet fly us into Barcelona. We all hooked up at the airport and came right to the hotel."

Four inches shorter than Sabrina but no less resilient, Devon had only recently learned to trust her heart again. She owed that to the man who followed her into the suite. Cal Logan was nothing if not persuasive.

"Hi, Caroline." His electric blue eyes skimmed her face. "You okay?"

She had no answer for that. Not with Rory's six- or seven-step seduction plan still wadded in her fist. At her helpless shrug, Cal patted her shoulder.

"Don't worry. Whatever the problem is, we'll help you fix it."

Completely overwhelmed, she stuffed the crumpled paper in her pocket and turned to the fourth new arrival. "You must be Marco."

The drop-dead gorgeous Italian surgeon who'd swept Sabrina off her feet—literally!—less than a month ago smiled an acknowledgment.

"I am indeed. It's good to finally meet you. 'Rina has told me a great deal about you."

"Same here."

Now that Sabrina knew Caroline was alive and still kicking, her belligerence returned with a vengeance. Rounding on Rory, she let fly with both barrels.

"When Caro told us you were the bastard who got her pregnant back in high school, I offered to fly to Spain and deliver a swift kick to your gonads. If you've hurt her again, or involved her in some kind of illegal activity, she's got four friends here who will take immense pleasure in following through on my initial offer."

Rory lifted a brow and glanced from her to the trio

standing shoulder-to-shoulder with Caro. His gaze lingered briefly on Devon, assessed Cal and Marco, swung back to the woman facing him with both fists planted on her hips.

"Thanks for the warning," he said, not sounding unduly concerned. "You're Sabrina Russo, right? Dominic Russo's daughter?"

"How did you… Oh, that's right. You're in the spook business."

"Personal security," he corrected mildly. "And you're Devon McShay."

It was a statement, not a question, but Dev responded with a nod.

"You want to introduce me to your friends, Ms. McShay?"

"This is Cal Logan, CEO of Logan Aerospace."

"Which recently acquired Hauptmann Metal Works in Dresden," Rory commented. "I saw the write-up in the *Wall Street Journal*." His glance shifted to Marco. "And…?"

"Dr. Marco Calvetti," Sabrina supplied. "Aka His Excellency Don Marco Antonio Sonestra di Calvetti, Twelfth Duke of San Giovanti, Fourteenth Marquis of Caprielle and a bucketful of other titles I haven't gotten down yet."

She tossed back her hair and glared at Rory.

"Introductions over, Burke. Now would you and/or Caroline kindly tell us what the hell is going on?"

Eleven

Room service arrived before either Rory or Caroline could comply with Sabrina's demand for an explanation.

While the waiter set up the *tapas* and uncorked the wine, Rory headed for the bedroom to exchange the hotel's plush terry-cloth robe for some clothes. He returned a few moments later wearing jeans and a black polo shirt.

Caro debated changing, as well, but the robe covered her from neck to midcalf. And the aromas rising from the array of appetizers were generating some embarrassing noises from the vicinity of her stomach.

"We haven't eaten since…" She had to think. "Yesterday."

"Sit," Sabrina ordered, pointing a stern finger. "You can talk while you eat."

"There's more than enough for all of us. Everyone, help yourselves."

"First things first," Rory stated. "I need something stronger than wine."

Sabrina gave a huff of impatience, but when he brought a bottle of scotch and glasses over to the coffee table both Marco and Cal signaled their approval.

The men dragged chairs over to form a semicircle around the food and drinks. After everyone had a glass in hand and Caroline had filled a plate with a selection of appetizers, Sabrina infused her voice with exaggerated politeness.

"Now?" she asked.

"Now," Rory agreed. "But before we start, I need your assurance that what we're about to tell you doesn't leave this room."

"Why?"

"It hasn't hit the papers yet. With luck, it won't before Interpol has a solid lead on the kidnappers."

"Kidnappers?" Devon gasped.

She was seated on the sofa next to Caroline. Her brown eyes flooding with dismay, she laid a quick hand on her partner's arm.

"You were kidnapped?"

"Not me. One of Rory's clients. Or rather, a prospective client. We met with him a few days ago here in Barcelona. Elena—his wife—contacted Rory right after she got the call from the kidnappers. We were on the way to the airport and made a swift U-turn."

A stark silence followed. Cal Logan broke it by setting his scotch on the coffee table with a thud.

"Let me get this straight, Burke."

Caroline knew Cal had played football in college. According to Devon, the aerospace CEO could also be as ruthless as the next man when it came to business. But none of the three women had ever seen him square his shoulders and look so intimidating.

"Your prospective client is kidnapped," he said, his tone dangerous, "and you drag Caro into the middle of it?"

Marco wasn't any happier. His dark brows snapped together, and his voice cut like a scalpel. "You should have put her on a plane immediately, Burke."

"I don't know about your women, gentlemen," Rory drawled, "but mine has a mind of her own. The only way I could have put Caroline on an airplane was to hog-tie her and stuff her into a suitcase."

The possessive pronouns generated instant and very diverse reactions from the women they'd been applied to. Sabrina snorted at the blatant sexism. Devon shook her head. Marco and Cal turned toward Caroline.

She chose to ignore their speculative glances. *And* the unspoken question of her relationship with Rory.

She needed time to sort through that crazy business about his so-called operations plan before she could answer that. Instead, she speared a spiced onion from her plate and downed it before sharing more details of the frightening ordeal.

"Rory and a team from Lloyd's of London negotiated with the kidnappers, in coordination with the Spanish authorities and Interpol. Rory delivered the ransom yesterday afternoon. Juan—the man who was taken—and his driver weren't released until late last night. Or I guess it was early this morning. I've kind of lost track of time. I'm not even sure what day this is anymore."

"What an awful thing for you to go through," Devon commiserated.

"It wasn't as bad for me as it was for Juan's wife, but I'll admit those were the scariest forty-eight hours of my life." Her eyes lifted to Rory. "Especially after you strapped on a gun and went to deliver the ransom."

"They were a little tense for me, too," he admitted with magnificent understatement. "You did a helluva lot more than stay on the sidelines, though. Elena couldn't have gotten through the most terrifying forty-eight hours of *her* life without you, sweetheart."

He'd done it again. Staked another claim too obvious to ignore. Caro flushed but refused to acknowledge the casual endearment.

"Yes, well, I'm just glad it's over."

"No kidding!" Sabrina muttered.

Setting her plate on the coffee table, Caro slewed sideways to face her partners.

"I received some up-close-and personal training on executive security this week. Given the kind of clients EBS caters to, we need to take a hard look at how we would respond if one of them is kidnapped."

The comment shot Cal upright in his chair. "Respond, hell!"

"I didn't mean we would shoot it out with kidnappers. But Dev and Sabrina and I need to look at how we would protect ourselves if we're with a high-risk client and something happens."

"From what 'Rina has told me of your business," Marco said, frowning, "all of your clients are high risk."

That was true. The three men in the room were prime examples.

"Something we'll definitely have to think about," Sabrina agreed, her mind clearly on other matters. "Marco, why don't you and Cal go down to the lobby and see about getting us rooms? Take Burke with you."

"No need for me to go," Rory commented with a dry look at the blonde. "I already have a room."

Immune to sarcasm, she flapped a hand. "Then have a drink in the bar with the guys."

"Please," Dev said a little more politely. "Sabrina and I would like to talk to Caro."

She could guess what they wanted to talk about. The subject of their conversation was sitting directly across from her, waiting for her to call the shots on this one. Slowly, she nodded.

"The triumvirate has spoken," Cal said as he rose with an easy grace that belied his size. "Come on, Burke. I want to hear more about your business."

"And your assessment of the risks to our women," Marco added as the men headed for the door.

When it closed behind them, "their women" rolled their eyes. Sabrina's and Devon's expressions held a touch of resigned amusement, but Caro's morphed quickly into wariness as her friends made themselves comfortable. Obviously, they weren't going anywhere until they got some answers. Caroline wished she had some to give.

"I can tell this is going to be a long session," she conceded. "Dev, pour us another glass of wine while I load up our plates. We'll eat, drink and gab."

"Just like we used to."

For a moment the years seemed to melt away. They could have been college juniors again, snuggled up in their tiny apartment in Salzburg to discuss men, plans for the weekend, the latest museum Devon had dragged them to, the city's upcoming international music festival and classwork—usually in that order.

Time and maturity hadn't altered the priority, Caroline acknowledged with a rueful smile as she bit into a garlic-flavored olive. Men still topped the list.

"It's just us girls now," Devon announced unnecessarily as she followed Sabrina's example by kicking off her shoes and curling her legs under her on the sofa. "What's the deal with you and Burke?"

"Okay, here goes." Caro pulled in a deep breath, blew it out. "I followed your advice, Dev, to trust my instincts and see where they took me. In short order, they took me to…"

She held up a hand and ticked off the tumultuous events of the past week, one by one.

"The hottest sex I've ever had. A romantic Valentine's Day dinner under the stars. A guitarist playing flamenco music. An emerald and diamond ring. A marriage proposal. Another night of hot sex. A kidnapping. A…"

"Whoa, whoa, whoa!" Sabrina jerked upright. "Back up there, missy."

"To?"

"To the ring."

"And the marriage proposal!" Dev exclaimed.

"I was as shocked as you are," Caro admitted. "I totally didn't see it coming, although Rory and I agreed the sex was great. Okay, spectacular. Then he said almost exactly what you said, 'Rina."

"Oh, Lord! What did I say?"

"It has to mean something that the spark is still there after all these years. Since I was most definitely feeling the heat, that struck home."

Frowning, Caro speared a shrimp swimming in

curry sauce. Reducing everything that had happened between her and Rory into a few sentences took concentrated effort.

"He also reminded me he's been on his own since he was sixteen. He's decided it's time for a wife. Kids. Someone to come home to," she finished quietly.

"So tell him to get a dog," Sabrina declared without a shred of sympathy.

Devon responded more slowly. "What about love, Caro? I know it's hard to believe it can grow so quickly, but Cal and I are living proof. Sabrina and Marco, too. Maybe Rory fell hard after seeing you again. Maybe his proposal came from the heart."

"I wouldn't have such a hard time believing that if I hadn't found a copy of his operations plan."

"His what?"

"Here it is." She pulled the crumpled paper from the pocket of her robe. "Operation Caroline Walters. Read it and weep. I almost did."

Sabrina sprang out of her chair. Her sun-streaked blond curls brushed Dev's dark red bob as she leaned over her partner's shoulder.

"Scope out the *target!*" she exclaimed. "Is that you?"

"Evidently."

"Arrange contact," she read incredulously. "Initiate contact." Her brows soared. "Ensure appropriate restitution?"

Caroline let out a long breath. "Rory told me right

up front that he always pays his debts. He also said he intended to make things right with me."

"By marrying you?"

"I guess. Maybe. Oh, hell, I don't know. I found that piece of paper, like, two minutes before you guys knocked on the door. I haven't had time to absorb all the implications yet."

She shoved a hand through her hair, struggling with a whirlwind of emotions.

"My first instinct was to throw his damn plan in his face. Then I remembered all the trouble he went through to arrange that ridiculously romantic dinner. And how good he was with Elena. And how I go up in flames whenever he takes me in his arms."

Talking through her confusion helped, Caroline realized. A lot!

"And now all I can think about is how I felt when he left to deliver the ransom. The terror almost ripped me apart. I swear to God, I couldn't breathe the whole time he was gone."

"Well," Devon said after a long silence. "That pretty much answers how you feel about the man. The question now is whether he feels the same about you."

"I know he wants me. I *think* he loves me. In Rory's mind, they're the same thing."

She looked at each of her friends in turn. The three of them had shared so much. So many highs, such devastating lows. Now Sabrina and Devon had found the loves of their lives. They *had* to know the answer to the question still gnawing at Caro's heart.

"Is he right? Do want and need and love add up to the same thing?"

Five stories down, Rory was nursing his second scotch of the night.

So were Cal Logan and the doc, but they hadn't gone almost twenty-four hours without eating. Nor were they coming off the adrenaline rush of recovering a client from kidnappers. And they hadn't just had the damn rug yanked out from under their feet because of a minor misunderstanding.

The scotch was biting into Rory's empty stomach. So were frustration and a growing sense of indignation.

"I mean, what's the problem with making a plan?" he threw at the other two men.

Logan was sprawled comfortably in one of the hotel's lounge chairs. He was wearing a business suit, but he'd stuffed his tie in his pocket and popped the top two buttons of his white shirt.

The doc—he'd told Rory he preferred that to the string of titles Sabrina had rolled off—was more casually dressed in slacks, a thin sweater and a suede bomber jacket. Evidently the tawny-haired witch he'd fallen for had barely given him time to change out of his scrubs before hustling him to the airport in Rome.

Both men had regarded Rory with undisguised hostility at first. In the past half hour, however, their hostility had given way to a rueful sympathy that only fueled his indignation.

"What's wrong with devising a plan?" he asked again, feeling aggrieved. "I knew what I wanted and went after it. You'd think Caroline would appreciate all the effort I put into finding her and setting up our reunion."

"You'd think," Logan agreed.

"I didn't intend to pull my people in for a conference until later this year. I moved up the schedule and set the meeting here in Spain to give her company the business. It wasn't just a ploy to get to her," he insisted. "EBS made a bundle off that conference."

The doc swirled his scotch. "I doubt the company's bottom line concerns Caroline at the moment. Or 'Rina or Devon."

"Yeah, well, it should. I checked their financials. EBS didn't start showing a profit until they landed Logan here as a client."

"They secured another big client this morning," Calvetti announced calmly. "With all the worry over Caroline, Sabrina hasn't finalized the details yet. But it appears EBS has been chosen to work the International Neurosurgical Institute's annual convention in Milan."

"And that's another thing!"

Scowling, Rory thumped his glass on the table and glared at the other two.

"Caroline says Logan here has Devon tied up working exclusively for his corporation. You talked Sabrina into opening an office in Italy. I suspect you'll *keep* her in Italy by feeding her more conventions like the one in Milan."

"That's certainly my intention."

"So where does that leave the third partner in their enterprise? Jetting all over Europe to handle the remainder of EBS's business? I'm here to tell you, gentlemen, it ain't gonna happen."

"How do you figure to make it 'un-happen'?" Cal Logan asked curiously. "Or has that objective bit the dust, along with the rest of your op plan?"

"I haven't given up on the plan. Not completely. Although looking back, I see now I might have made a tactical error in proposing to Caroline so soon."

"Might have?" Logan echoed dryly.

"I really thought I'd set the scene." Frowning, Rory tried to decide how his carefully scripted evening had gone wrong. "Dinner under the stars. Music. Candles all the hell over the place. Most women would have…"

Even before he finished the sentence, it hit him. Caroline wasn't like most women. The women he knew, anyway. She'd taken what life had thrown at her without complaint and emerged with a quiet, unshakable strength.

She didn't need Rory to protect her or shield her, much less atone for past sins by making her financially secure for the rest of her life. What she needed…what *he* needed was to put the past where it belonged. In the past.

"Hell! I've got this all ass-backward."

His chair almost toppled over as he shoved out of it.

"I'm going upstairs. Without an escort," he added when the other two started to rise. "I'll send Devon and Sabrina down here."

"Good luck with that," Logan drawled, settling back in his chair.

When Rory stepped out of the elevator, he came face-to-face with the two women he'd been prepared to eject from his suite.

"Caroline sent us to find you," Devon said. "She wants to talk to you."

"Good. I want to talk to her, too."

He tried to read their expressions for an indication of what he would have to deal with when he hit the suite. The redhead's face was carefully neutral. The blonde, on the other hand, didn't try to disguise her feelings. Her earlier belligerence was gone, but she issued a challenge so fierce that it seared the air.

"You've got this one chance to get it right, Burke. A slim chance. Don't screw it up."

Her expression softened for a moment. Just long

enough to give Rory a glimpse of the woman who could inspire such passionate loyalty in her friends and bring a cool customer like Calvetti to his knees.

"Good luck."

He nodded his thanks and strode down the hall. By the time he'd unlocked the door to the suite, he'd marshaled his arguments and put them in priority order.

Every damn one of them flew out of his head when he spotted Caroline. She was standing at the window, her hands shoved in the pockets of her robe, her gaze fixed on the illuminated spires of that character Gaudí's masterpiece.

The sound of the door closing brought her around. "I've been thinking."

"So have I."

"Maybe…"

"Wait, Caroline. Let me go first. Please."

At her nod, he crossed the room. "Your friends warned me I had only one chance. They also warned me not to screw it up. The fact is, there's no way I could screw things up any more than I already have."

"You think so?"

"I know so." He shook his head, wondering how the hell he could have been so dense. "I thought I could cover all the options. Work out the details in advance. The problem is, I was working from an outdated database. You didn't… You *don't* fit any of my prescripted parameters. You're not the girl you were then, Caroline, any more than I'm the hot young stud I thought I was."

She gave him a ghost of a smile. "Young? No. Hot? Well…"

"What I'm trying to say is that I see now I've made a mess of this. My only excuse is that I've never been in love before."

Surprise flickered across her face. Moving swiftly to take advantage of it, Rory raised a hand and cupped her cheek.

"I know, I know. I fed you a load of crap about not knowing the difference between lust and love. I discovered the difference real fast when you found that damn op plan. I thought I would lose you. Thought I *had* lost you. Then your friends burst onto the scene, and I had to stand there with my guts hanging out."

She bit her lip. "That's…that's one way to describe love."

"Here's another." Bending, he brushed her lips with his. "I want to be part of your life, any way you'll have me, for as long as you'll have me."

When he raised his head, the tears shimmering in her green eyes slammed into him like a fist to his chest.

"Christ! You have to believe me, Caroline. I never meant to hurt you."

"I know."

The tears came faster, spilling freely. Rory's heart hit the carpet with them. Cursing his clumsiness, he swiped his thumb across her cheek.

"It's okay. Don't cry, sweetheart. I understand. I blew it."

"You idiot!"

He flinched, then melted with relief when she broke out in a radiant smile.

"These are tears of joy."

She threw her arms around his neck, grinning and sniffling at the same time.

"I love you, too. I knew it before we left the Casteels' house, but that idiotic plan threw me off balance. I just needed a little time to talk through the shock. Sabrina and Dev helped with that."

"I owe them," Rory said fervently. "Big-time. And I always…"

"Pay your debts," Caroline finished, laughing. "We've already had this conversation. Several times. Let it drop, and kiss me instead."

Rory was more than willing to comply. When they came up for air, however, he insisted on resolving one final matter.

"I know I said I'd give long-distance courtship a try, but we've already let too many years build up between us. Marry me, Caroline. Tonight. Tomorrow. The day after, if you need time to shop for a dress."

He was back, Caro realized with a hiccup of mingled laughter and chagrin. The take-charge Rory who'd steamrolled into her life after so many years.

"What about blood tests?" she protested. "A

license? And wouldn't we need to ask someone from the U.S. Consulate to witness the ceremony?"

He had the grace to look embarrassed for a moment.

But only a moment.

"I, uh, already planned for those contingencies. Just say yes, and I'll take care of the details."

Oh God! She loved this man. She had, she realized with a pang of sharp, piercing joy, since that long-ago summer when their lives first collided.

"Yes," she said, surging up on tiptoe to cover his face with kisses. "Yes, yes, yes, *yes!*"

Twelve

At the vehement insistence of Devon and Sabrina, the wedding took place three days later.

They demanded the extra day to add the small touches Rory hadn't factored into his plan. Like six solid hours spent roaming Barcelona's exclusive boutiques. And a full afternoon in an exclusive spa to pamper the bride.

At *Caroline's* vehement insistence, the wedding was conducted on the beach at Tossa de Mar.

Harry Martin took care of flying Caro's mother to Spain. She sat in the front row with Sondra Jennings, looking slightly dazed by the fact that she wasn't in Kansas anymore.

A dozen or so GSI operatives filled the folding chairs behind them. Across from them sat Captain Antonio Medina and a sprinkling of the resort employees Caroline had worked with during the week of the conference.

Elena and Juan Casteel were there, too. They'd arrived several hours early so Elena could come up to the bride's room and "lend" her an exquisite lace mantilla.

"Something borrowed, something blue," she said with a smile. "That's the custom in your country, isn't it?"

Since Caro had decided on a simple, off-the-shoulder white satin dress and a wreath of white baby's breath in her hair, Elena draped the mantilla around her hips.

"You and Rory are right for each other." Her eyes misting, she tied the ends in a loose knot. "Like Juan and me. I hope you have as many happy years together as we've had."

Caro enveloped her in a fierce hug. "I hope so, too."

The mantilla fell around her hips in graceful folds as she took Harry Martin's arm to walk from the hotel to the beach. The retired cop had risen to the occasion. In Caro's admittedly biased opinion, he looked like an older and *very* sexy version of James Bond in his white tie, tux and Ray-Bans.

"I told you Rory was a good man," he said with a grin.

"So you did."

At the first, sultry notes of a flamenco, Harry escorted Caro down the steps to the beach. Sabrina and Dev preceded them. They'd indulged their individual tastes as bridesmaids. 'Rina's backless, strapless dress in eye-popping red turned every head in the rows of folding chairs. Devon was more subdued but every bit as stunning in pale lavender. The color had a special significance for her. Something to do with ski suits and headbands. Sabrina and Caro didn't quite get the connection but promised faithfully to adopt the color for Dev's wedding to Cal in May. Sabrina's would take place just a few short weeks later.

For a giddy moment, the three friends had contemplated a triple ceremony. All for one and one for all. In Salzburg, of course, where they'd first met.

Rory had gulped and made an obvious effort to rein in his impatience to get Caroline to the altar. Aid came from an unexpected quarter when Marco suggested that his mother the duchess would be very unhappy if he and Sabrina didn't have their wedding at the family's palazzo in Naples.

So here Caroline was, floating on Harry's arm, with the sun sparkling on the Mediterranean and Tossa's medieval castle brooding in the distance.

And there stood Rory, aligned alongside Marco and Cal. All three looked impossibly handsome in their tuxes, but Caroline had eyes for only one man. In the space of a few weeks he'd shocked and confused and confounded her. Yet all she had to do was see the wind ruffling his hair and the smile in his amber eyes to know Elena had it right. She and Rory had been meant for each other from the moment they'd met.

Her heart singing, Caroline gave thanks for her past as she went eagerly to her future.

* * * * *

*Celebrate 60 years of pure reading pleasure
with Harlequin® Books!*

*Harlequin Romance® is celebrating by showering
you with DIAMOND BRIDES in February 2009.
Six stories that promise to bring a touch of sparkle
to your life, with diamond proposals and dazzling
weddings, sparkling brides and gorgeous grooms!*

Enjoy a sneak peek at Caroline Anderson's
TWO LITTLE MIRACLES,
*available February 2009
from Harlequin Romance®.*

'I'VE FOUND HER.'

Max froze.

It was what he'd been waiting for since June, but now—now he was almost afraid to voice the question. His heart stalling, he leaned slowly back in his chair and scoured the investigator's face for clues. 'Where?' he asked, and his voice sounded rough and unused, like a rusty hinge.

'In Suffolk. She's living in a cottage.'

Living. His heart crashed back to life, and he sucked in a long, slow breath. All these months he'd feared—

'Is she well?'

'Yes, she's well.'

He had to force himself to ask the next question.
'Alone?'

The man paused. 'No. The cottage belongs to a
man called John Blake. He's working away at the
moment, but he comes and goes.'

God. He felt sick. So sick he hardly registered the
next few words, but then gradually they sank in.
'She's got *what?*'

'Babies. Twin girls. They're eight months old.'

'Eight—?' he echoed under his breath. 'They must
be his.'

He was thinking out loud, but the P.I. heard and
corrected him.

'Apparently not. I gather they're hers. She's been
there since mid-January last year, and they were born
during the summer—June, the woman in the post
office thought. She was more than helpful. I think
there's been a certain amount of speculation about
their relationship.'

He'd just bet there had. God, he was going to kill
her. Or Blake. Maybe both of them.

'Of course, looking at the dates, she was presum-
ably pregnant when she left you, so they could be
yours, or she could have been having an affair with
this Blake character before…'

He glared at the unfortunate P.I. 'Just stick to your
job. I can do the math,' he snapped, swallowing the
unpalatable possibility that she'd been unfaithful to
him before she'd left. 'Where is she? I want the
address.'

'It's all in here,' the man said, sliding a large envelope across the desk to him. 'With my invoice.'

'I'll get it seen to. Thank you.'

'If there's anything else you need, Mr Gallagher, any further information—'

'I'll be in touch.'

'The woman in the post office told me Blake was away at the moment, if that helps,' he added quietly, and opened the door.

Max stared down at the envelope, hardly daring to open it, but when the door clicked softly shut behind the P.I., he eased up the flap, tipped it and felt his breath jam in his throat as the photos spilled out over the desk.

Oh, lord, she looked gorgeous. Different, though. It took him a moment to recognise her, because she'd grown her hair, and it was tied back in a ponytail, making her look younger and somehow freer. The blond highlights were gone, and it was back to its natural soft golden-brown, with a little curl in the end of the ponytail that he wanted to thread his finger through and tug, just gently, to draw her back to him.

Crazy. She'd put on a little weight, but it suited her. She looked well and happy and beautiful, but oddly, considering how desperate he'd been for news of her for the past year—one year, three weeks and two days, to be exact—it wasn't only Julia who held his attention after the initial shock. It was the babies sitting side by side in a supermarket trolley. Two identical and absolutely beautiful little girls.

* * * * *

When Max Gallagher hires a P.I. to find his estranged wife, Julia, he discovers she's not alone—she has twin baby girls, and they might be his. Now workaholic Max has just two weeks to prove that he can be a wonderful husband and father to the family he wants to treasure.

Look for TWO LITTLE MIRACLES
by Caroline Anderson,
available February 2009
from Harlequin Romance®.

CELEBRATE
60 YEARS
OF PURE READING PLEASURE
WITH HARLEQUIN®!

We'll be spotlighting a different series
every month throughout 2009
to celebrate our 60th anniversary.

Look for Harlequin® Romance in February!

**Harlequin® Romance is celebrating by showering
you with Diamond Brides in February 2009.**

Six stories that promise to bring a touch of sparkle to
your life, with diamond proposals and dazzling weddings,
sparkling brides and gorgeous grooms!

Collect all six books in February 2009,
featuring *Two Little Miracles* by Caroline Anderson.

*Look for the Diamond Brides miniseries
in February 2009!*

www.eHarlequin.com   HRBRIDES09

HARLEQUIN® Romance®

This February the Harlequin® Romance series
will feature six Diamond Brides stories featuring
diamond proposals and gorgeous grooms.

Share your dream wedding proposal and you could WIN!

The most romantic entry will win a diamond
necklace and will inspire a proposal in one of
our upcoming Diamond Grooms books in 2010.

In 100 words or less, tell us the most romantic
way that you dream of being proposed to.

For more information, and to enter
the Diamond Brides Proposal contest, please visit
www.DiamondBridesProposal.com

Or mail your entry to us at:

IN THE U.S.: 3010 Walden Ave., P.O. Box 9069, Buffalo, NY 14269-9069
IN CANADA: 225 Duncan Mill Road, Don Mills, ON M3B 3K9

You're invited to join our Tell Harlequin Reader Panel!

By joining our new reader panel you will:

- Receive Harlequin® books—they are FREE and yours to keep with no obligation to purchase anything!
- Participate in fun online surveys
- Exchange opinions and ideas with women just like you
- Have a say in our new book ideas and help us publish the best in women's fiction

In addition, you will have a chance to win great prizes and receive special gifts! See Web site for details. Some conditions apply. Space is limited.

To join, visit us at
www.TellHarlequin.com.

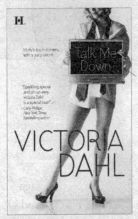

REQUEST YOUR FREE BOOKS!

2 FREE NOVELS PLUS 2 FREE GIFTS!

Passionate, Powerful, Provocative!

nocturne™

USA TODAY bestselling author

MAUREEN CHILD

VANISHED

Guardians

Immortal Guardian Rogan Butler
had no use for love, especially after his
Destined Mate abandoned him. So when beautiful
mortal Allison Blair sought his help against a
rising evil force, Rogan was bewildered by the
undeniable electric connection between them.
Besides, his true love had died years ago,
and it was impossible that he could even
have another Destined Mate—wasn't it?

Available February 2009 wherever books are sold.

COMING NEXT MONTH

#1921 MR. STRICTLY BUSINESS—Day Leclaire
Man of the Month
He'd always taken what he wanted, when he wanted it—but she
wouldn't bend to those rules. Now she needs his help. His price?
Her—back in his bed.

**#1922 TEMPTED INTO THE TYCOON'S TRAP—
Emily McKay**
The Hudsons of Beverly Hills
When he finds out that her secret baby is really his, he demands
that she marry him. But their passion hasn't fizzled, and soon their
marriage of convenience becomes very real.

**#1923 CONVENIENT MARRIAGE, INCONVENIENT
HUSBAND—Yvonne Lindsay**
Rogue Diamonds
She'd left him at the altar eight years ago, but now she needs him
in order to gain her inheritance. Could this be his chance to teach
her that one can't measure love with money?

#1924 RESERVED FOR THE TYCOON—Charlene Sands
Suite Secrets
His new events planner is trying to sabotage his hotel, but his
attraction to her is like nothing he's ever felt. Will he choose to
destroy her...or seduce her?

**#1925 MILLIONAIRE'S SECRET SEDUCTION—
Jennifer Lewis**
The Hardcastle Progeny
On discovering a beautiful woman's intentions to sue his father's
company, he makes her a deal—her body in exchange for his
silence.

#1926 THE C.O.O. MUST MARRY—Maxine Sullivan
Their fathers forced them to marry each other to save their
families' fortunes. Will a former young love blossom again, or
will secrets drive them apart?